VIRAGO
MODERN CLASSICS
442

Angela Carter

Angela Carter (1940–1992) was born in Eastbourne and brought up in south Yorkshire. One of Britain's most original and disturbing writers, she read English at Bristol University and wrote her first novel, *Shadow Dance*, in 1965. *The Magic Toyshop* won the John Llewellyn Rhys Prize in 1969 and *Several Perceptions* won the Somerset Maugham Prize in 1968. More novels followed and in 1974 her translation of the fairy tales of Charles Perrault was published, and in the early nineties she edited the *Virago Book of Fairy Tales* (2 vols). Her journalism appeared in almost every major publication; a collection of the best of these were published by Virago in *Nothing Sacred* (1982). She also wrote poetry and a film script together with Neil Jordan of her story 'The Company of Wolves'. Her last novel, *Wise Children*, was published to widespread acclaim in 1991. Angela Carter's death at age fifty-one in February 1992 'robbed the English literary scene of one of its most vivacious and compelling voices' (*Independent*).

By Angela Carter

Fiction
Shadow Dance
The Magic Toyshop
Several Perceptions
Heroes and Villains
Love
The Infernal Desire Machines of Doctor Hoffman
Fireworks
The Passion of New Eve
The Bloody Chamber
Nights at the Circus
Black Venus
Wise Children
American Ghosts and Old World Wonders

Non-fiction
The Sadeian Woman: an Exercise in Cultural History
Nothing Sacred
The Virago Book of Fairytales (editor)
The Second Virago Book of Fairytales (editor)
Expletives Deleted

SHADOW DANCE

Angela Carter

A *Virago* Book

Published by Virago Press 1995

Reprinted 1997

First published by Virago Press 1994
First published in Great Britain by William Heinemann 1966

Copyright © Angela Carter 1966

All rights reserved. No part of this publication may be
reproduced, stored in a retrieval system, or transmitted in any
form or by any means, without the prior permission in writing
of the publisher, nor be otherwise circulated in any form of
binding or cover other than that in which it is published and
without a similar condition including this condition being
imposed on the subsequent purchaser.

A CIP catalogue record for this book is available
from the British Library

ISBN 1 86049 041 7

Printed and bound in Great Britain by
Clays Ltd, St Ives plc

Virago
A Division of
Little, Brown and Company (UK)
Brettenham House
Lancaster Place
London WC2E 7EN

1

The bar was a mock-up, a forgery, a fake; an ad-man's crazy dream of a Spanish patio, with crusty white walls (as if the publican had economically done them up in leftover sandwiches) on which hung unplayable musical instruments and many bull-fight posters, all blood and bulging bulls' testicles and the arrogant yellow satin buttocks of lithe young men. Nights in a garden of never-never Spain. Yet why, then, the horse-brasses, the ship's bell, the fumed oak? Had they been smuggled in over the mountains, in mule panniers? Dropped coins and metal heels rang a carillon on the green tiles. The heels of her high boots chinked as she came through the door.

'Morris!' she said.

He, in a vacant muse, turned; and flinched away from her, from the touch of her hand on his arm, in a sudden terror.

'Hellooo, Morris,' she said; her long vowels moaned like the wind in pines. 'I thought I might see you here.'

'Oh, God in heaven,' he said in his mind, as if invoking protection against her.

'Shall I buy a drink for you, Morris? Have you no money? Always penniless, poor Morris.'

He had half thought, half imagined what she would look like when he was forced to see her again but, meeting her with this unprepared suddenness, he could not speak or think or look at anything but her face. So he stared at her, and she stared back at him. Beseechingly, did she stare beseechingly?

She was a very young girl. She used to look like a young girl in a picture book, a soft and dewy young girl. She used to look like the sort of young girl one cannot imagine sitting on the lavatory or shaving her armpits or picking her nose. She had such a little face, all pale; and soft, baby cheeks and a half-open mouth as if she was expecting somebody, anybody, everybody she met to pop a sweetie into it.

And she had long, yellow, milkmaid hair and her eyes were so big and brown they seemed to gobble up her face, as those of a bush baby do. They were as big as the eyes of the dog with eyes as big as cartwheels in the fairy story; and as brown as wood or those painted on Egyptian mummy cases. And her darkened lashes swept down over half her cheeks.

And she was so light and fragile and her bones so birdy fine and little and her skin was almost translucent. You wondered how she had the strength to hold the great, big, heavy half-pint mug when she drank and you remembered how the red wine had seemed visible, running down the white throat of Mary, Queen of Scots, as she drank. A month ago, she was a beautiful girl; how could such a girl not be beautiful?

The scar went all the way down her face, from the corner of her left eyebrow, down, down, down, past nose and mouth and chin until it disappeared below the collar of her shirt. The scar was all red and raw as if, at the slightest exertion, it might open and bleed; and the flesh was marked with purple imprints from the stitches she had had in it. The scar had somehow puckered all the flesh around it, as if some clumsy amateur dressmaker had roughly cobbled up the seam and pushed her away, saying: 'I suppose it will do.' The scar drew her whole face sideways and even in profile, with the hideous thing turned away, her face was horribly lop-sided, skin, features and all dragged away from the bone.

She was a beautiful girl, a white and golden girl, like moonlight on daisies, a month ago. So he stared at her shattered beauty. The noise in the public house banged at his head; pulses behind his eyes began to throb and beat. The white walls waltzed around him and he thought he might faint. But he did not faint.

She used to come here, every night; but she drank little – she only used to have her little half pint to last her a whole evening, a modest, temperate, unassuming little half that she would buy for herself, to demonstrate her independence. She would use it to mark her place at a table when she made butterfly darts across the crowd to settle lightly at someone's table, smiling her tremulous, shy, disingenuous smile and saying 'Halloo' with the dying fall of an F. Scott Fitzgerald chick spinning giddily to hell; and she gathered them up in armfuls, her lovers, every night, in the manner of a careless baby playing in a meadow, pulling both flowers and grass and nettles and piss-the-beds in a spilling, promiscuous bundle.

'She is a burning child, a fiery bud,' said Honeybuzzard, before he knifed her. All the clichés fitted her; candle-flame for moths, a fire that burned those around her but was not itself consumed. And now her face was all sideways and might suddenly – at too large a mouthful of drink or a smile too unwisely wide or a face-splitting request for 'bread and cheeeeeeese' – leak gallons of blood and drown them all, and herself, too.

'I have lots of money, Morris, if you would like me to buy you a drink.'

Her voice had the asexual music of dripping water, cold and pure, each word clear and distinct, a separate drop dripping on your head so that after a time you thought you were going mad, as in the old-world Red Indian tortures; but you could not close your ears to her. She used to speak with the electronic, irresistible sing-song of a ravishing automaton; now her voice gave the final, unnerving resemblance to a horror-movie woman to her.

'See, I will buy you a whole pint.'

And the bride of Frankenstein looped her hand through Morris's arm to lead him to the bar but still he said nothing, though he shuddered at his linked nearness to her. He struggled vainly for words, a greeting; finally, thank God, he found he was able to speak her name. Her bare, naked name; but it would do, for a start.

'Ghislaine.'

The bad spell on him began to break for he had always disliked and resented her name and he found he disliked and resented it still. Ghîslaine. With a circumflex over the 'i' when she signed her letters. And she herself habitually pronounced the 'h' when she told you her name; it was as though she was clearing her throat but what she was doing was telling you her name. Ghislaine. Rotten, phoney Ghislaine. He looked down at the top of her head in pure, remembered dislike.

'I didn't,' he said, clear and audible now even though his tongue rolled in his mouth like a frightened frankfurter, 'I didn't know you were out of hospital.'

'I came out of hospital today, in fact, Morris.'

She was always introducing the name of the person with whom she was speaking into her conversation. Her talk was a kind of present, gift-wrapped, tied with shiny, red-ribbon bows, sealed securely and addressed to only one especial person. An evening's chat with her entailed the reception of a whole Christmas of carefully chosen and wrapped presents just for you alone. To talk to her, simply, made you feel pampered, loved and wanted. Or had done, until a month ago.

'See, I have ample money to buy bitter for you.'

She drew a handful of loose notes, brown and green, from the pocket of her jeans with a gesture of childish pride that was supposed to be very naïve and touching and, indeed, was so useless one had seen it several times before.

'You see, I saved so much on living expenses when I was in hospital,' she explained and smiled; which was ugly.

A shiver went down him and when it subsided the muscles of his back continued to squirm and twitch with apprehension. Why was she being so matter of fact, as if she had gone to hospital to have a wart cut off her foot or her tonsils out? What good did she think it would do her with him?

Thank God, there was no room for them to sit down, close to each other. They stood at the bar and were continually separated for whole, gratifying minutes by the pushing and buffeting tide of customers. He sipped cautiously at his beer. And was suddenly gripped with the nauseating conviction that it tasted of her.

He was drinking her down sacramentally; the taste of her metallic deodorant sweat and the foundation cream she smeared over her lips to make them pale and a chemical smell of contraceptives and her own sexual sweat. At once the memory of her naked, threshing about beneath him, homed to him like a pigeon and horrified him with its impropriety. He felt as though he had had an erection at a funeral. He could not bear to drink from his glass again and flushed it behind a bowl of melting ice, to hide it.

'I mustn't get upset,' he thought fearfully; he thought he might start screaming, with fear and hysteria, snatching up things and throwing them around.

She said: 'Isn't it funny. It wasn't even properly spring when I went to the hospital, the trees were only just a little bit green at the tips and it got dark so early. But now it's almost summer and everywhere is so lovely and waaaaarm.'

Oh, the lingering voice on the long vowel, like an intimate caress. A caress from a witch-woman.

'The sap's rising,' he said. His voice shook. Now, he wondered, why did I say 'The sap's rising' to her? What will she think I mean?

She glanced at him over the rim of her glass, sharing sly secrets, and laughed her personalized, patented laugh – she must be the only girl, anywhere, who could laugh like that. The shimmery, constricted yet irrepressible giggle of a naughty little girl, such a young, lovely and wicked giggle.

'She is trying to carry on, then, as if nothing has changed,' he thought.

But everything had changed. The bar was full of her friends but none of them would say a word to her because they knew (or thought they knew) about the scar and why she wore it. They were all staring at her but nobody greeted her. Cruel backs pushed past her and sharp elbows dug into her and when the brown glow of her regard caught a face half turned towards her, that face swung away immediately.

There was the corpulent Oscar, who laid her (while his wife was bearing their third child, as in *Streetcar named Desire* – life imitating rotten art again, as Honey always said it did) in his marriage bed. And Henry Glass, whose ordered loneliness she shattered and left him alone again to pick up the pieces as best he could. And little brown Bruno, whom she had out of curiosity and who never had a woman before or since. To name but three.

And they all looked the other way when they thought she was looking at them.

But they were all very excited. The bar buzzed with rumour and surmise; they quivered with curiosity and the frenzied strain of seeming to mind their own business while they concentrated on attending to hers. They gibbered with expectation because they thought Honeybuzzard would come in, soon, and there would be a confrontation and such a scene, such a scene.

They were disgusting. Morris was disgusted. Powered by disgust of them, Morris forced himself to turn to her and at last chat almost naturally on neutral topics. About the clement weather and the possibility that he was gestating a cold in the head. Then, when he felt he was finally in command of the situation, she asked after his wife, with a chilly sweetness.

Edna. Oh, the bitch, to ask after Edna. He thought of Edna, red-eyed, dishevelled, moaning: 'If you ever go near that woman again, I shall kill her, for I love you, my love. But I love you.'

And only, he remembered bitterly, the one time; just the once, and hardly worth the emotional price he had paid for the temporary possession of the white body and all this long, yellow hair writhing over the pillow like crazy snakes. All this long, yellow hair that hung, now, quiescent, down her shoulders to her waist; and when she half-turned to stub out a cigarette her back, shining with her tumbled hair, seemed to be plated to the waist in gold, like a holy image.

Edna's hair was brown, a lifeless brown.

It was nearing twenty past ten. Honeybuzzard was in the habit of arriving at the public house at something after ten and he was oddly set in one or two habits of this kind. He was unlikely to appear tonight, now it was so late. So there would be no scene, no fight. But the crowd's excitement was still increasing. A glass smashed A girl started crying, tearing with her nails at fat Oscar. A man vanished, clutching his mouth to the gentlemen's lavatory.

He thought that Ghislaine must have come in to wait for Honeybuzzard also. She would want to weep and glitter with public tears and fatten her undernourished little self on them, her poor little vanity, all pale and thin with pinman Oxfam arms and legs. There would be an orgy of emotion, with blows and tears and violence, all about her and she would bulge fatly on it. She only asked after Edna in the hope of getting a crumb or two of sustenance for her starved little self-respect. He decided to act coolly and calmly.

'Edna is quite well, really. But she is suffering under one of those bad headaches that she has, tonight, and cannot leave her bed.'

'Poor thing! Such agony!'

He glanced involuntarily at the scar. He thought how much it must have hurt her.

Then she said: 'And me . . . don't try and tell me you can ignore it. I can see it in your eyes, as if it were reflected. Is it so very bad? Is it as bad as it seems, when I see it in your eyes? Am I so very ugly?' She inched forward, gazing up at him until she was almost leaning against his breastbone. Her voice went on and on.

'Am I as ugly as I fear I am? It's still so very red and raw and there were all sorts of complications. I couldn't keep from peeling off my bandages to look at it and they kept hiding the mirrors from me, wasn't that cruel, Morris? And at first it would not even try to heal up but kept on running, all blood and yellow stuff.'

He closed his eyes. 'You must be brave,' he said and was glad when he saw she had not heard him. She veered sharply away from what she herself said; she could not linger on anything, not even on her own pain. She was not calm nor matter of fact, not at all; it was a pose she could not sustain.

'You look just the same, though, Morris.' As if this followed naturally on what she had just said. 'It's funny, that I should think you might change just because I have.'

'Oh, Ghislaine.'

'You still look like an El Greco Christ. So many men with black beards do, of course, especially when they are all thin and bony, like you are, Morris. But it is more than that, it is something in your eyes. Though I don't want to look in your eyes, for fear of what I might see.'

'Here we go again,' he thought. He felt for cigarettes. A twinge of pure embarrassment shot through his excruciating pity and lingering fear. He was being served with an emotional Neapolitan ice tonight, three flavours; it was too rich for his tender stomach. A wave of faintness swept over him and he clung to the bar, sighing.

'And Edna, is she still crucifying you, Morris? That completes the picture, that accounts for the look in your eyes, doesn't it, Morris?'

She had always been a very embarrassing girl. She would say things like: 'Why does your mouth look so dead, Morris?' or, intensely, 'Why are you always acting a part, Honeybuzzard?' in a shockingly brutal and frank way, in the manner of young girls with high pitched voices in plays about unhappy marriages among the lower middle classes such as are broadcast on the Home Service on Wednesday afternoons. She thought she was shocking people; in fact, she was only embarrassing them.

She would say: 'I lost my virginity when I was thirteen,' conversationally, as she lit a cigarette, or she would complain of the performance of her last partner, or she would ask you if your wife satisfied you sexually and your pale, replying smile she would assume to be shock and distress and then she would giggle her little giggle. Or she would describe her menstrual pains; and he remembered the graphic recital of a course of treatment for a vaginal discharge.

The scar was like a big, red crack across ice and might suddenly open up and swallow her into herself, screaming, herself into herself. She did not give him time to reply, did not even allot him the customary moment of stunned silence she, in the past, had always allowed for after such a remark. She veered, immediately, back into her own misery.

'It was terrible in hospital. I was in this ward with all these old ladies and they were all dying and they kept on saying what lovely times they'd had when they were young. It was awful, Morris.'

He tried to heave his pity back into the foreground of his mind with a tremendous effort for she was unbalanced and sick and in pain; she didn't realize what she was saying.

'Have you anywhere to go tonight, though?' he asked.

'Shall I go home with you, Morris? Is that what you are saying?

'I didn't mean – oh, no, I didn't mean –'

'And shall we make love, like last time, Morris? If Edna is ill, she wouldn't hear, if we stay in the front room –'

'Ghislaine, please –'

'Is it so horrible, then; am I so horrible?'

'Time,' said the publican and all the lights went out. Irresponsible Morris. Heartless Morris. *Sauve-qui-peut* Morris. He had had enough. He went out with the lights. In the interstices of time in which they were dimmed, he slipped noiselessly away from her out into the liquid dusk and leaned against the wall for a moment, panting hard. It seemed he had been undergoing strenuous physical exertion. A car, roof down, filled with young people laughing and drinking from bottles, went by; he hated every unknown one of them.

'I hope you crash!' he shouted after them. One boy heard him, turned round and threw a bottle crookedly back at him. The car vanished in a renewed burst of laughter. The bottle smashed in the gutter at Morris's feet. He stared unbelievingly at the splinters of glass. Dregs of brown liquor spilled and gleamed like the shiny backs of a nest of disturbed beetles running over the stones.

'They meant that for me,' he wondered.

He felt the bottle shattering against his face and, raising his hand, was bemusedly surprised to find no traces of blood from a gashed forehead on his fingertips. Why not? In a metaphysical hinterland between intention and execution, someone had thrown a bottle in his face, a casual piece of violence; there was a dimension, surely, in the outer nebulae, maybe, where intentions were always executed, where even now he stumbled, bleeding, blinded . . . He walked on in a trance, scarred like her.

Though, nursing his invisible cut, he was at first not aware of it, it was a remarkable and romantic night. There was a deep blue, secret and mysterious sky with a low, white satin moon appliqued on its bosom and the voluptuous shadows of the city trees moved with black shadows. Morris walked quietly and his footfalls made small, private noises, as if he was the last man left alive in the whole world. Pit, pat, his footsteps, one, two.

He began to pretend there was nobody alive but himself and everyone else was dead. The fantasy grew into a conviction; the invisible cut healed up and vanished. The empty houses appeared to him like rocks or cliffs, the parked cars at the roadside abandoned shells of deep-sea creatures, Pearly Argonauts or giant sea snails. Then, to his distress, an owl, hooded in a tree, hooted. He wondered if he ought to let the owl live. It hooted again, a lonely, travelling sound like a train going away, far, far away.

An answering hoot came from a blind window in the middle of a shabby terrace. A series of hoots, at first wavering and uncertain, finally triumphantly imitative. Some wakeful child was at his bedroom window, playing at being an owl. The child and the real owl conversed gravely together, without understanding but with diplomatic formality, like emissaries.

So there was an owl alive, and a child and Morris stopped trying to pretend that everyone was dead. Horribly, he returned to the real world.

She. She would have turned to find him gone. Well, then, what business was it of his? He did not care what happened to her, who it was she finally found to comfort her, if she found anyone. The fresh green breath of the night moved and shivered around him and chilled him to the bone. He was afraid when he heard footsteps behind him; was she coming after him, like a Fury . . .?

He went past the padlocked and deserted cemetery. Honey said he found her weeping and injured in the abandoned cemetery, with her shiny black raincoat torn open and she all naked underneath it, brutally exposed, like a skinned orange; but Honey told lies. But in the dimension where Morris was blinded with broken glass there she lay, on the rank grass, all tears and blood and his heart stopped for a second at a rustling, a stir in the bushes. But it was a cat who sprang through odorous lilacs and balanced on a wall and spat at him.

He went past the nursing-home where his wife would be having a baby, if she could have her way. Past the park where teenage lovers moaned and writhed in the rhododendron bushes, among the fag ends and dogshit. Past the dazzle of city light below, where the hill sloped steeply down to the dark ribbon of the river.

He was sure, now, that Ghislaine was not following him, in spite of his nervous apprehensions and the ghosts he saw; so he could go home. Home. High in a decaying old house where Edna lay in a darkened room, a poor flat fillet on the marble slab of her bed. She moaned when light spilled through the open door from the tiny hallway.

'Sorry. Sorry, darling.'

He could just make out her pale face smudging the pale surface of the pillow with a darker pallor. He asked her how she was, perfunctorily.

'Oh, all right.' She was a liar. Unfairly, he was angry with her because she was minimizing her sickness. 'All right, really,' she said. 'Did you have a nice time?' Her poor, thin, ghostly, little, grey voice, drifting out in sad stops and starts.

'No, not very. I . . . there was . . .' His own voice trailed away. He decided not to tell her about Ghislaine, not yet; he would wait until she was better. And then, but then, would she understand?

'Can you possibly get me a little cup of coffee, Morris? Black coffee?'

Glumly, he realized that, at heart, she did not care where he had been and to whom he had spoken; she was too ill, the headache standing on her brain like a huge, heavy man who, perhaps, occasionally jumped up and down in metal-spiked boots. But she synthesized an interest, good wife that she was; and besides, how could she ask a service of him unless she indicated how little account she took of her own needs and feelings in relation to his actions and feelings?

'Oh, yes,' he said weakly, 'of course.'

He spooned powdered coffee into two cups. As he turned the gas tap, he thought, 'always one way out.' He had a brief mental picture of Edna, in the morning, coming into the gas-filled room, choking and parting the air with waving hands, finding him huddled on the floor, dead and blue in a pool of vomit. He lit the burner. The gas under the kettle was disturbing, it flared and whined, very bright, very loud; a dragon seemed to be snoring in the dark kitchen. He was glad when the coffee was made, the gas turned out and he was alone once more. Edna wanted aspirins with her coffee.

'Please, love, couple of aspirins . . . thanks, love.'

They were very free with endearments to each other, and with other politenesses. For example, she thanked him profusely for the drink and he supported her weak body so that she could manage the mug as she gulped it down. Her brown head against his shoulder felt light as a dead branch.

After a moment, she said, 'Morris, darling, Honey has been. He left a message. He's going to London.' The little words came out by slow, painful ones. When she had a headache, she talked carefully, cautiously, as one walks on an icy road.

'Oh. Oh, no. Did he say where he would be staying?'

'No.'

'Or for how long he would be away?'

'No.'

'Oh, God!'

'Darling, I'm sorry, but don't shout out like that — my head . . .'

'No, I'm sorry. I'm thoughtless. But I didn't, you see, want to go into the shop . . . not for a while. And with Honey away — but did he not even hint how long he would be away?'

'Not the tiniest hint, no.' She sighed, a miniature sound

indicating long-suffering weariness. What a brute he would be to go on questioning her.

'Did he, did he say anything else at all?' Morris thought furiously that Honeybuzzard must have heard of Ghislaine's return and treacherously left him alone to cope with the consequences. Briefly, he wanted to kill Honeybuzzard.

'I only saw him for a moment, Morris, dear, and he just said that he was going to London. I only saw him for a moment.' There was the ghost of a reproof audible in her voice, now, because he had started to nag her.

'Of course, of course. But –'

'Oh, Morris, not now! Please!' She turned over on her face, to shut him out. He was a brute, an insensitive animal; she meant nothing to him, her illness was nothing to him.

Chastened, he took his own coffee into the living-room and carefully closed the door behind him. He stumbled over the rough rush matting and a pile of books beside the long, wicker chair thudded and crashed over the floor. He froze; he imagined each sound intolerably magnified in the tender sounding-box of Edna's skull. But she did not call out. Perhaps she had gone to sleep, already? Or did she fear he would go on questioning her if she revealed she was still capable of calling out?

In a fever, he stared around the room as if it were a stranger's room. White walls, sanded floor, a painting of orange forms on a pink ground – he turned his eyes hurriedly away from it. They focussed on a bookshelf in the corner, where hung a low, red-shaded lamp. He could not stop looking at the bookshelf.

Guiltily, he crept up the room, edging slowly, reluctantly, peering over his shoulder and around him anxiously, as though he was scared someone was watching him. He tingled with apprehension lest the unlikely happened and Edna came out of her bed on noiseless feet to see what he was doing, or the impossible happened and Ghislaine materialized in a black mist to blast him to hell for what he was going to do.

He was taking down a book from the shelf, one of a history of the French Second Empire in twelve volumes which he and Honeybuzzard, high on tea, had bought for an outrageous price at an auction when they were thinking, for a time, of concentrating on second-hand books. Edna, Morris knew, had never touched even so much as the cover of one volume; which was just as well, for, tucked beside a sepia and white photograph of Napoleon III, was a black envelope with a red lining which contained a number of pictures of Ghislaine.

She and Honeybuzzard spent a whole afternoon working on these pictures. The room above the shop which he and Morris ran together was all scarfed in darkness but for a battery of electric lights gathered together from all sorts of places, focussed on the shiny brass bed, and the work had been punctuated by cries and exclamations as they tripped over the network of trailing flexes. It was November and the gas fire hiccupped and farted and her buttocks grew mottled purple and crimson as she squatted naked before its glowing cones between takes, as if she was offering herself backwards to Mr Therm. After each pose, she would glance questioningly up at the two men with the silent question: 'Am I being wicked enough?' Her face was sweet, white, innocent and childish, like ice-cream.

Honeybuzzard liked to wear false noses, false ears and plastic vampire teeth. An ithyphallic Honeybuzzard, retaining only his habitual dark glasses and a wide variety of false noses, false ears, vampire teeth etc. appeared in a number of the pictures. Morris himself had declined to be featured with her or them both, although both of them had urged him; he was afraid that Edna might one day discover the photographs and Honeybuzzard mocked him cruelly for this. But he stood firm.

Tirelessly, Ghislaine contorted herself, spread herself wide, arrayed herself in a bizarre variety of accessories. Honey would disappear at intervals to the shop and return with his arms full of new toys. Military boots and a brocaded hat; rhino whips; clanking spurs; a stag's head; a dappled, gilded, flaking fairground Dobbin from some dismantled roundabout on which they both rode, her giggle, her springtime giggle, coming in spurts.

The images of the two lovely, strong, young bodies had a certain strange and surreal beauty; but Morris could not associate these pictures of her with his own burning recollection of her flesh at all. *'Memento mori,'* he said to himself. A quotation floated from a vague corner of his mind. '"Besides, that was in another country, and the wench is dead." Who said that?'

He thought he ought, in decency, to burn up all the pictures. She would like to be remembered as she had been, though – yet decency dictated that she should be destroyed. But he could not burn the pictures, for the fireplace was already dismantled for the summer and equipped with a large jug of dried cow parsley or meadowsweet. Morris could not think of how he might improvise a fire without disturbing Edna.

Finally, he searched around for the pot of Indian ink; he intended to blot out her face in each pose, as they do in newspaper photographs of men in prison. He thought that would duly extinguish her. Yet, once he had the pen in his hand, he found he was finely, carefully, striping each image of her with a long scar from eyebrow to navel. All the time, he wondered why he was doing it; it seemed a vindictive thing to do and he had never thought of himself as a vindictive man. But he did not stop until he had finished marking them all in. When he looked at them spread all round his feet to dry, he was filled with revulsion at himself.

'I don't know what came over me, your honour,' he appealed

to an invisible magistrate accusing him of perpetrating an obscenity. And now there was nothing to be done but put them all away again.

Overcome with weariness, he lay down on the musty cushions of his wicker chair and reached for his coffee; but it was cool, by now, brackish and, anyway, far too sweet. His carious teeth shrieked in protest at the first sip and he pushed the mug away; he was to be denied even that comfort, then. He was tired, so tired; he felt his eyes closing.

'It is wrong of me to go to sleep,' he thought. 'I should stay awake and think of what I should do. There must be something I can do, about her.'

But he was terribly weary; he ran out of himself at every pore and the black sleep ran into him, face down on the cushions. So he slept, but not for long, for he had bad dreams. He dreamed he was cutting her face with a jagged shard of broken glass and blood was running on her breasts not only from her but from himself, from his cut head. There was a gallery of people watching them, and applauding sporadically, like the audience at a cricket match; among them he made out Honeybuzzard and Edna, both smiling and nodding their heads. And then he and Ghislaine were in his own bed and her head rolled on the pillows and all the yellow hair went brown, as if it was blighted, and then it was Edna he saw that he was slicing open and there was blood everywhere, on her and on his hands and in his eyes and mouth. A voice repeated over and over: 'There is too much blood.' He realized, after a time, that it was his own voice.

He woke up, sweating. The moon had set and the room was black dark. His heart beat so loud, so strong that it seemed to shake his veriest foundations. He thought in despair: 'How can I manage with Honey gone.'

After that, he thought: 'Am I so useless that I cannot face anything without Honey, or somebody, to help me?' And grimly acknowledged that this might be true, that he might be totally impotent, helpless, useless as the junk in his shop.

He thought of his shop, filled with junk, with rubbish. With broken chairs, chipped crockery, piles of unread, unreadable books, the thrown-out, decaying, shabby, worn, moth-eaten, stale rubbish, rank with misery. 'I am,' he thought grimly, 'a second-hand man; and she, now, is a second-hand woman.'

They would put her in the window arranged on a rug or a sofa, with a label Sellotaped to her navel: 'Hardly used.' With a dome of immortelles beside her. And the dust would snow down, in time, and obscure her face entirely, and mice would nest in her guts (as they had done in the grand piano), and no one would ever stop to look at her but an incurious dog who paused, leg cocked, to pee against the wall, and himself, eyeing his own shop window anxiously, to see if she had moved.

His shop, his dreadful shop. Edna would sometimes pathetically tell new acquaintances that her husband was in the antique business. This small pretension touched and grieved him and he would feel sorry for her and almost loving towards her. But sometimes she would say 'he is a painter', depending on how she had assessed the character and personality of the person to whom she spoke. And then Morris would feel desolate and betrayed and come nearest to hating her. For, yes, he painted; yes, he painted pictures. But, no, he was a bad painter and knew himself to be a bad painter and the desire to be a painter and the knowledge that he would never be a good painter burned inside him all the time. It was his secret, his fatal secret, which she – out of a naïve desire to impress – would tell to the whole brutal and uncaring world.

He thought as a painter, dreamed as a painter, defined himself as a painter. He could best accommodate the thought of

Ghislaine as the subject for a painting, a Francis Bacon horror painting of flesh as a disgusting symbol of the human condition; that way, she became somehow small enough for him to handle, she dwindled through the wrong end of the telescope of art. Yet he could only think in this way, never execute; never paint the painting which would justify treating her as a thing and not a human being.

When he signed his name on a picture, he experienced a sense of defiance and exhilaration, as though he was throwing down a gauntlet to the world; and then he would shiver to see the worthlessness of the gesture, of the thing itself, and would stack his picture, still wet, face to the wall in the slip of a room at the shop in which he worked. He could hardly bear to look at his pictures, once they were done. But Edna, poor, uncomprehending Edna would insist on sorting out one or two the shapes and colours of which pleased her and, in spite of his entreaties, would take them home and hang them on the walls of their flat. Perhaps she regarded them as some sort of visible justification for the hardships she bore for them. So the pink and orange abstract glowed from the wall at him like an accusation of his own inadequacy, although it comforted his wife.

She liked him to be a painter; she was proud of him. Her faith was touching and entire. She had even painfully acquired a few phrases of painters' jargon and pained him by using them indiscriminately to all sorts of people. But in the end he had not the heart to stop her or to clear the flat of his paintings for she had few pleasures, so very few pleasures: only the pleasure of enduring stoically his moods and his lovelessness for the sake of the himself she was the only one who could see. Yet why did she love him? Why did she go out to work to earn money to keep him? Why did she slave away to keep the flat fresh and bright and pretty (those weeds in the fireplace, and hand-thrown pottery mugs, and towels with fringes and roses on them, and his socks so neatly darned)? Why, why?

When the room was running with her imaginary blood?

(And also with his own; and with Ghislaine's. He wondered if he would drown in it.)

2

But he survived the night and the morning was as bright as a new penny. He decided not to go to the shop at all that day, but, instead, to go to the auction sale. Making a decision, even such a small one, eased his mind and he bought his cigarettes with a light heart, chatting freely about the weather to the man in the shop. Morris lingered outside the shop, perspiring gently in the fresh heat of the spring sun, inhaling the first dizzying lungfuls of smoke and idly re-reading the notice-board; there was one especial card, '15-year-old girl seeks riding lessons, own jodhpurs', which had been slowly browning there for the best part of two years at the rate of threepence a week, which was what the tobacconist charged for display. He had fleeting but disturbing fantasies about her, a panting, wet-lipped nymphet with jutting nubile breasts, flourishing her crop and crying 'Faster! Faster!' As his wife never cried.

There were, he saw, kittens available, black, black-and-white and tabby. Would Edna like a kitten? A kitten for a child surrogate? For she longed for children or, rather, as she said so often, for *his* children. A kitten, though, would be something for her to love, for all women loved helpless furry things that tottered on impetuous, infirm, infant legs and in imperious, high-pitched voices demanded love. And, he thought hopefully, a furry lovable kitten might siphon some of her affection away from himself.

He knew that women like Edna could give their hearts and souls to cats and kittens, if nothing else was forthcoming. If he had not married Edna, she would have aged into a cat-spinster in a bed-sitter where every available space was covered with milk-saucers and chopped-chicken saucers and the air was rank and thick with cat-piss and the carpet covered in a snow-drift of hair (black, black-and-white, tabby). A kitten, then, for Edna. Edna. He had accidentally summoned up the image of Edna; a shadow crossed the sun.

Barely recovered, black rings around her eyes like a silent film comedian, she had dragged herself off to the assembly line of the cigarette factory while he weltered in guilty sleep. She would be home in time to prepare his supper. He stamped out his cigarette, half-smoked, in sudden fury because she was ill and uncomplaining; and then was seized with compunction because he was gratuitously wasting her hard-earned pennies. And who better than he to know just how hardly they were earned?

The auction sales were held in the gutted corpse of what had once been an Edwardian department store, where tall, thin pillars topped with fading garlands of gilded leaves insinuated hints of departed elegancies among the heaped junk around them and strangely placed long mirrors, flyblown, in dark corners, suddenly astonished you with your own, speckled reflection. It was quiet, dark and soothing. Morris sucked up eagerly the smell of dirt, poverty and graveclothes; blindfolded, he could have recognized the smell of an auction sale. He loved the smell.

He loved junk. He loved to nose questingly among the abandoned detritus of other people's lives for oddments, fragments, bits of this and that. When he was confronted with a pile of discarded uselessness, he would worry it and tease it like a happy dog with an enormous bone, until he had extracted every drop of pleasure or profit that he could from it. The best times of his life were the dark nights when, in Honeybuzzard's van, they went secretly to the deserted, condemned old houses which the city council planned shortly to demolish and, by the light of guttering candles, would sort over and pick about in all their dead flotsam.

'Nothing special, today,' said the white-overalled porter, a hard-faced, strong-shouldered cynic who could nightly be seen drinking away his tips and bribes in the furtive public house two doors away. Morris was pleased to be on such confidential terms with the porter for it was an outside confirmation of himself in the role of an antique dealer. Today, then, he would be an antique dealer; it was another decision.

'You never know,' he returned in as professional a deadpan as he could and turned to crawl on hands and knees among the heaps of crockery on the floor, turning over each chipped cup or coverless tureen to inspect the mark on the bottom.

Suddenly his attention was caught and held by a number of vividly coloured plaster gnomes among a pile of bent saucepans. The feet of the gnomes were caught in the loopings of an uncoiling plastic clothes-line, as if someone had lassooed them with it. Under the table, grass-stains still on their bases, one gnome perched on a plaster toadstool, smiling with idiot glee; another perched on a huge plastic daffodil of the most vibrant yellow, grasping in a cruel fist a plaster butterfly and laughing with sadistic relish; a third pushed a plaster wheelbarrow laden with a surprising trove of broken tea-pot lids and plastic clothes-pegs while a fourth flung himself down on a plot of plaster grass in an attitude of Dionysiac abandon, propped on a debauched plaster elbow. They were painted in bright, crude colours – red

24

jackets and green trousers and superbly white beards. All the paint all over them, from tip of their black hoods to toe of their high, brown boots, gleamed as if it was new and fresh.

Morris wondered what domestic catastrophe would make a man sell even the plaster gnomes from his garden. It was a horrid piece of evidence for mutability; Mutability, goddess of the auction room, dusty-fingered Mutability, the old-age-pensioner goddess. And she ruled over the casserole containing the half-empty packet of sugar no one would ever finish, now; and the dropsical white tea-pot with the brown tidemark left in it by years of tea-making by dead women in flowered aprons (withered and dead, all the chintz flowers); over all the odd, disjointed fragments of other people's lives.

He picked up a little, sharp, broken knife out of a tray of knives and forks. The little knife with its handle worn to the grooves of generations of fingers must have had one specialized, esoteric function in a certain household but the key to its use was now lost for ever and might only be guessed at. Had it been used only for hewing chunks of iron-hard Parmesan? Or opening oysters, in the good old days, when an oyster went into every working man's steak-and-kidney pudding? Or for cutting intransigent bootlace knots when father's Saturday-night-fuddled fingers balked at them? But no one would ever know.

Beds with the shallow depressions in them that men and women, like rivers, mould out for themselves over the years. And piles of photographs of other people's darlings, smiling from outmoded clothes in forgotten summers at Torquay and elsewhere. And books signed inside, with love; up for sale, now, dead love for sale. And in such an atmosphere of hope decayed Morris was at home. He was picking up and examining a small, white jug with a curious face moulded, leering, beneath the lip, when a heavy hand crashed on his shoulder.

'The big boys will be after that, Morris; put it down, put it down. It will cost far too much for you, dear boy, and besides, who would you sell it to?' The fat man, Oscar, laughed, grinding his fingers in Morris's flesh.

'You never know,' responded Morris, moving away, but the other swayed forward with him, still laughing. Oscar was always laughing, though he seemed only rarely amused. Morris wondered if he kept a laughing machine in his guts, switched on all the time to electronically simulate hilarity. 'There is room for it in his gut,' he thought. 'And room for a midget to live there, a midget technologist to look after it. And the postman could push his little mail through Oscar's navel . . .'

'Leave it to the professionals, dear boy, the professionals.'

Morris, lost in his dream, wondered for a second why Oscar was saying this; then realized the fat man was mocking him.

'What am I, if not a professional?' he said huffily, painfully defending the suave, the suede-jacketed and Chelsea-booted image of himself as an antique dealer.

'You're learning the trade.'

'I've been running a shop for two years, now –' But he gave up in the face of the other's contempt. Now Oscar shrugged away the topic dismissively and drew closer. He lowered his voice to a confidential bellow, a bull rhino talking secrets. Morris tingled with apprehension.

'Why did she engage you in conversation last night?' asked Oscar, low and urgent.

Morris took a deep breath and set his jug down beside two blue cups and saucers and a cracked Chinese bowl. He traced his finger up and down the scarlet dragon upon it and remarked, with tremendous composure: 'What a covetable lot this is! I should very much like this bowl – look at the curly dragon. And the cups may well be early Spode.' (He thought anxiously, 'Am I overdoing it?')

'Tell me, why?' repeated Oscar, disregarding the antique-dealer act completely.

Morris sighed. 'I don't know. I know nothing at all.'

'Why hasn't she gone to the police?'

'How should I know?'

'You were close to her at one time.'

'So were you.' They looked at one another for a moment; then, at the same time, both turned away.

The auctioneer mounted his kitchen chair, drank from his glass of water and cleared his preparatory throat. The motley assembly gathered around him, as around an open-air-preacher. Morris and his companion drew automatically to the group, mingling with the fried-fish smelling old ladies with American cloth shopping bags shopping for God knows what; and the bargain hunting housewives all stern and businesslike; and the hand-in-hand young couples nervously setting up house together and a bit furtive about it as if they had a placard round their necks saying: "We are making preparations to sleep in the same bed." And the supercilious dealers, whose voices, as they whispered secrets together, sounded like the rustling of five-pound notes.

The litany began sluggishly. Morris discovered after a few minutes that he had bought, almost by accident, a glass case of moulting stuffed pigeons for twenty-five shillings. They seemed very cheap. He warmed to them because no one else wanted them. But Oscar rolled with laughter beside him.

'Fancy buying that rubbish!' He jabbed his thick, derisive forefinger at the glass case. The birds stood knee-high in shed feathers; they looked emphatically dead, the work of a ham-handed and amateur taxidermist. Oscar's derision only made Morris like them the more since Oscar was a Design Centre obsessive, a contemporary clean lines and white paint man, who lived in a Scandinavian living box and stuffed his dustbins weekly with old, shabby, broken things for they meant nothing to him. Morris thought Oscar classed Morris among such things and would have put him away in the dustbin if he got the chance, cramming the lid firmly down on his faint cries.

He immersed himself comfortingly in a pile of books, sinking deeply among a great many ancient calf-bindings that left traces of disintegrating leather on his hands. The bidding went on in a bagpipe drone. There was a sepia picture in one book of Orpheus leading Eurydice from Hell. Orpheus carried a harp to show who he was. Orpheus had a very straight nose and a lot of curls. Eurydice had one breast hanging out of her draperies and a perturbed expression since she was just about to vanish because Orpheus' head was poised on the turn, already. Morris thought Orpheus was a fool, in the first place, to want to go and retrieve the silly bitch. Then Oscar nudged him.

Raising his eyes, he saw Ghislaine in the doorway with bright day behind her, outlining her; the sun shone on her great mound of golden hair.

Again, he took the coward's way out, slipping into the street while she knelt to look at a pile of framed pictures. Morris running down the street, saw a future before him in which he would be always running away from Ghislaine. Wherever he went, she would be sure to follow, like Mary and the little lamb of nursery rhyme fame, and he Mary. Even if he spent all his time in gentlemen's lavatories, if he locked himself in the large wardrobe in his hitherto private bedroom or took the train to London to join – say – the Brigade of Guards, and hide beneath a feathered helmet, sooner or later, Ghislaine would arrive.

Descending, a water nymph, from the cistern; or magically inhabiting a shirt on his hangers ('it looks so much better on a man' – he shuddered); or he, on his high, haughty horse, under the weight of his traditionally concealing panoply, would see her picking her delicate way among the whirring cameras of American tourists and she would throw to him the clinging white poison flower of her hand and smile in horrid greeting.

And he would start running, as he was running now. His breath came painfully and he began to see red discs in front of his eyes. He was not used to running; but, he thought grimly, he would probably get used to it in time. Through the red discs, he saw, to his astonishment, that Oscar was chugging indomitably beside him and put on a fresh burst of speed. But Oscar was a healthy man and kept pace with him easily. They ran on abreast, scattering pedestrians. In this way they covered a surprising distance together.

'Let's have a small snack,' suggested Oscar as they came into the centre of the town.

Painfully furling his limbs, limp, yielding, spent with exertion, Morris found himself obediently entering the café with Oscar. 'Why am I doing this?' he thought in perplexity. He cast about for a reason and, not finding one, comforted himself: 'Perhaps Oscar will buy me a cup of tea.'

When Morris first came to the town, the back-room self-service cafeteria of this café was panelled in grained wood and the chairs and tables were solid and immovable oak. Everything had been coloured a nutritious brown, then. The slow years passed.

As they passed, the management finally decided to drag the place by its ears into contemporaneity. It was forced, against its will, to become a coffee bar.

The panelling went, to be replaced by chic, cream distemper and the heavy tables, covered with tablecloths worn, torn and brown and somehow comforting because so well used, were replaced by steel and plastic structures so light they had to be screwed into the ground to prevent them overbalancing at a touch. New chairs were introduced, covered with lemon yellow simulation leather that adhered to arse and thighs in warm weather, so when you rose you carried the chair with you, like a dog clinging with its teeth to the seat of your trousers.

Nevertheless, in spite of all these innovations, the primeval atmosphere of the place could not be exorcised. There remained a strong illusion of brownness. Inescapable, undisguisable brownness, dowsing over all with great ladlefuls of brown Windsor soup. In the back café, everything went brown. Defeated and acknowledging it, the management staffed the café with Struldbrugs.

Once women, as one could see by their dresses, but now withered away, their sex ground down by the stubbed-out cigarettes of the years, the life poured out of them into some slop-pail somewhere as if from thick, chipped teacups, these creatures patrolled ceaselessly the tables, seizing cups as soon as their contents fell below a plimsoll line visible only to themselves and wiping down Formica table tops with great, melodramatic sweeps of wet and filthy rags.

Oscar and Morris stepped over a Struldbrug genuflecting before a painted wall with a bucket beside her and a rag in her hand. At the counter, plastic oranges bounced on unseen currents in carboys of orange squash and great urns bubbled and gurgled behind a plastic showcase containing an oozing selection of cakes, pies, rolls and sandwiches, sheathed in Cellophane so that they looked not like real food at all but some miraculous product of modern synthetic technology.

Morris took a meringue from the display with a pair of metal tongs; using the tongs seemed an exaggerated gesture of respect towards the meringue, but he supposed there was a reason for it. To his annoyance, he found he had to pay for himself since

Oscar was negotiating for a toasted bun. The counter attendant was still, just, recognizably a woman – she had a wide breast and paint on her mouth. But how long could she last, there? She promised to send the buns to Oscar and began to toast them for him. Toasted buns were something of a ritual. Before they could reach the secluded table Morris wanted to hide at, a Struldbrug was there before them, singing to herself as she wiped an ashtray with her cloth.

She sang how the boy she loved was up in the gallery, smiling down at her and waving his handkerchief, and then she broke off to say, 'Good morning, darlings,' and pottered away, making inconclusive little swipes at chairs and tables with her cloth as she passed.

Morris smashed his meringue with a fork so that cream spurted across his plate. He liked to eat his meringues with a polite fork, like a little gentleman.

'Nothing,' he said, 'quite like a meringue for breakfast.'

Briefly he wondered whether he always chose himself a meringue in the morning café because in this way he could easily indicate to anyone who saw him that he was unique and unconventional. I eat meringues for breakfast because I am an eccentric. But why is it necessary for me to behave like an eccentric?

However, he was quite certain, without affectation, that he liked meringues, and forked away industriously. Breathing a sigh of pleasure, he found he had blown a white spume of atomized meringue into the air like a contented whale. He felt very much better; the after-glow from his running mingled headily with the glow at having escaped her once again, at least for the time being.

'Why were you running away from her, Morris?' Oscar filled his cup with sugar, stirred, smiled.

Morris choked for a moment. When he could speak, he said in as off-hand a manner as he could: 'I walked out on her in the Gloucester last night. I wouldn't want to see her again so soon after doing that to her. And why did you run away from her just now yourself?'

'I think she thinks she can impose on me and I don't want her hanging about my house, thank you, upsetting the wife and kids.'

'And I don't want that, just like you. Except we haven't got the children.'

A Struldbrug, grey hairband slipping forward over grey forehead, inched forward with a steaming, lidded, hotel silver dish in her hand. She lamented in a series of long, lonely vowels, hardly disturbing their flamenco wail with the soft knobs of consonants. ' 'ose buns! 'ose buns!'

'Ah, my buns.'

Morris looked at the old woman. With every step she took, she crept nearer to the grave and no one to throw roses on her or to sniffle into a black-edged handkerchief as the spadefuls of earth hit the coffin. The meringue, suddenly was white as whited sepulchres with dead men's bones inside them. He could no longer fancy his meringue.

'This place makes me sad, sometimes,' he said.

'You're far too sensitive, Morris. They do you a very good toasted bun.' Oscar peered with pleasure inside his silver dish.

Morris hoped passionately that a great big snake would jack-in-the-box out of the dish and bite Oscar dead. He hated Oscar, his wife and children, even the dog. But hot, buttered Oscar wallowed at the trough greasily unaware of the beam of hatred focussed on him. Morris pushed away the ruined meringue. He decided to go in first. He lit a big, masculine, self-assertive cigarette, girding himself for the attack.

'You've only come in here with me because you want to find out something, Oscar, and you think I'm feeble enough to tell you things. You want to know all sorts of lovely, gory details and you think you can squeeze them out of me.'

'Well, dear boy, I'm sure there's much more to it all than meets the eye.' Oscar wiped his fingers on a clean, white handkerchief. He always called Morris 'dear boy', with a sneer.

'But what's it to do with me? Or with Honey?' Morris said bravely.

Oscar slitted up his eyes and said smoothly: 'So you want me to believe it has nothing to do with either of you, the terrible thing that happened to Ghislaine? You want me to believe what Honey says, about the teenage gang and the old churchyard and Honey just happening to find her there? You want me to think that?'

'Is it so incredible?' Yes. Of course it was incredible. But why should Oscar not believe it? Wasn't Oscar British?

'Honey's a liar,' said Oscar flatly. 'Dear boy.'

'For God's sake, give the "dear boy" a miss!' broke out Morris furiously.

'Keep your voice down or the manager will throw you out and you haven't drunk your tea yet.' He spoke like a kindergarten teacher. Morris slowly sank back into his chair.

'She was asking for trouble,' he said in a disgruntled voice. 'Running around like she used to do, daft bitch, late at night, and nothing on under her mackintosh. She used to climb over the wall of the park and rush up and down in the moonlight without a stitch on. And she'd go into the churchyard with flowers, sometimes. She said she didn't want the dead people to feel neglected. And just sit there, till all hours. I'm surprised it never happened before, something like this attack.'

'Mind,' continued Oscar, as if Morris had not spoke, 'I'm sure you had something to do with it but I'd never accuse you of more than covering up for Honey. You're not the type to go around knifing girls, are you, Morris? But you are Honey's closest friend.'

'Am I?'

Well, was he? In spite of their shared jokes and their shared lives and shared pleasures, were they friends? Honeybuzzard slipped like a slim, blond porpoise through potential nets of obligation and affection. His cool, bland, shining self darted swiftly through the world on its premeditated, obscure course and he was golden and peachy and he bubbled with simple, schoolboy fun and he was incommunicado. Relationships ran off him like water off the proverbial duck's back.

'Honey and I are business partners,' said Morris. He thought how forlorn his voice sounded.

'And another thing. Do you remember how you gave her to Honey? It seemed so odd, somehow, at the time. I remember in the pub, the way you said: "Take her and teach her a lesson, Honey." And we all laughed. But it was odd.'

'Shut up, for Christ's sake!' screamed Morris. The steady probing hit a nerve at last. Oh, the childish spite of it, blaming her for the disaster of their one time – she so beautiful but never to be enjoyed, was that her fault? At the time, it had seemed so. And therefore Honey, who was as heartless as she, should have her, to show her what heartlessness meant. 'Revenge is a wild kind of justice. . . .' Who said that? But was it justice that she should go so scarred and her life ruined? He put his head in his hands and groaned out loud.

The singing Struldbrug sidled towards them, weaving her hands in her apron.

'All finished, dearie?' she said to Morris and tried to take his cup away. Weakly, he managed to restrain her but she pounced on his plate.

'Ooh, what a mess you made with your cake! Never seen such a mess!'

It seemed to Morris that she singled him out especially for her affectionate attention, treating him as he supposed a nanny might treat a naughty but beloved child. She must feel maternal towards him, for some reason. Perhaps, once, she had a child herself.

'Still,' she said, 'never mind.' When he made no response, she insisted: 'Never mind, eh? eh?'

'That's right,' said Morris, at last, faintly.

Oscar, whistling a tune to himself, prepared to leave. He was satisfied. Why? Morris had revealed something but he couldn't tell what it was nor why Oscar's black beard should waggle with such spry self-congratulation. Oscar's beard crisped and curled in an ecstasy of virile energy while Morris's own beard wandered, apathetic and untrimmed, up around his ears and cheekbones and petered out in a Quixotic fringe on the edge of his chin. Oscar's unbearable beard jigged up and down and his whiter-than-white teeth gleamed.

'And is the shop doing well?' he asked.

Morris wished he was the Demon Decay and could storm Oscar's ivory castles so that they would fall out one morning as he chewed his good-morning toast and clatter, like eroded, blackened clinker, all across the family breakfast table, to the babbling distress of the great-bosomed, gipsy-dark wife. Morris tried to gather himself together.

'The shop's all right. We get by.' He was on the defensive.

'It is such a bad site, too, down there in the slums. An antique shop in the slums.' He laughed sombrely.

Morris stiffened and replied more strongly; 'We are all right, there, thank you. Americans think it is all very quaint and Dickensian and we get lots of them there in the summer. Especially females. In Bermuda shorts.'

Oscar talks to me as if he were bear-baiting, he thought, or mocking the lunatics in an eighteenth-century asylum. Silly fellow, silly fellow. They all talk to me like that – why? why? Why do they make me a scapegoat? But he did not want to know why, or to think about it.

So he began to play one of his favourite games. He imagined himself going down to the station and buying a single ticket and getting on a train and going far away. Anywhere, as long as it was away; he did not wish to arrive at a destination. To travel hopefully is better than to arrive. The Struldbrug would sing a good-bye song for him and he would say good-bye to her because she sang for him and called her dear.

But he would not say good-bye to anyone else. Not to Honeybuzzard, even; and least of all to Edna. 'Just going to get some fags, Edna, I won't be a minute.' But he would be for ever. And he would creep, deliciously surreptitious, to the bus stop and the exhilarating ride to the station would be as sweet as a kiddy's stolen raspberry jam and the city would go on about its business unaware that he was leaving it and would never walk there again.

He lit a cigarette and he was sinking back against the dusty train cushions and blowing out luxurious smoke as he watched, with the deepest gratification, the city dissolve into his past, into the past, to join such cities as Troy, Carthage and similar myths.

'And give my regards to Edna,' said Oscar as he rose to go. Morris did not even notice him. He was sucked down into his dream – going, going, gone. The flat, the shop, the cafe, going, going, gone. The jam-jar full of turps and brushes. Gone. Himself, tall, dark, sad man in a green corduroy jacket. Gone.

Yet when he came back to the café out of his dream, he found himself trapped inescapably in the town, in a private circle of hell, locked to the memory of Ghislaine like Paolo to Francesca in Dante. There was the memory of her, waiting for him, and he left the café and, invisible old woman of the sea, all ugly and piteous, she went with him, clutching him with her white legs and her long, slender arms. Ghislaine.

'Take her and teach her a lesson.' His own remembered words rang in his ears, drowning the noise of the traffic or casual conversation or radio music. 'But I never meant that,' he told himself. 'I never meant to hurt her.' Over and over again, he tried to reassure himself. 'It was a joke, a sort of joke. I'm not responsible for what Honey did. No, surely not.'

But all the spring, she went about with him, weighing him down, although he never saw her in the real world. In the night, she laid her wet, invisible mouth on his and he woke up, choking. She sat invisibly third at the supper table between Morris and Edna, poisoning the food with her breath. When Edna took off her clothes before going to bed, there was Ghislaine, taking off her clothes, too, in an obscene parody strip-tease and laying her golden head down on the pillow and he would wake up to find her smiling at him.

'You're nothing to do with me,' he would say to the phantom. But it only made her cling more closely to him.

He grew haggard and depressed while the weather continued crazily perfect; even the sunshine treated him ironically. The town blossomed. In the streets and on the buses, people said to one another: 'Never such a spring,' the people who could see the blossoming. The Struldbrug in the café sang snatches of emotive popular songs about lilacs in bloom and love, flotsam and jetsam from time-when, time-never-again, and would stroke Morris' shoulder when she saw him, as if she sensed and sympathized with his unhappiness. He only went into the café either very early or very late, now, so that he might not run into anyone he knew and only continued to go there at all because of the old woman.

The atmosphere around her was warm; she seemed protective and benevolent. He found he was thinking about her from time to time, wondering what she had been like when she was a little girl or a young woman. What colour, for instance, had been her hair before it faded to no colour?

May progressed slowly. The white lilacs in the churchyard where Honey said Ghislaine had been raped and hurt browned at the edges and reeked of halitosis and finally dropped down dead.

3

At the best of times, spring hurts depressives. Morris now stayed indoors a great deal, to keep out of it as much as he could. He was in hiding from the real woman. It seemed to him that she was a vampire woman, walking the streets on the continual qui vive, her enormous brown eyes alert and ever-watchful, and the moment she saw him she would snatch him up and absorb him, threshing, into the chasm in her face. But he could not hide from the thought of her.

He toyed with the idea of talking to Edna about it and trying to make her help him with his burden but finally could not bring himself to do it. It seemed that Edna had not heard of Ghislaine's return from her own friends, for she did not mention her name to him though sometimes he wished she would do so of her own accord, and he could bring it out into the open.

He lived in a state of guilty fear, starting at sudden noises, frightened of shadows. He was tormented by a recurrent dream, a mutation of the nightmare of the first night. He dreamed he was cutting Ghislaine's face with a kitchen knife. The knife was blunt and kept slipping. Her head came off in his hands, after a while, and he cut her into a turnip lantern, put a candle inside and lit it through her freshly carved mouth. She burned away with a greenish light. That was all. But the inconsequence of the dream was peculiarly horrifying.

He would wake up, his hair stiff with sweat, to find Edna stirring softly beside him and the idea of Ghislaine somewhere in the room, maybe hiding behind the curtain where he could not see her, and he would insist to himself: 'But it can't be my fault! It can't be!' Yet he was still guilty.

He tried to keep the next day, the new day, away from him as long as he could, staying in bed pretending to be asleep long after the troubled night was over. When the morning was almost gone, the fear that she, the real one, might come knocking at his door overcame him and he would at last jerk out of bed, no longer able to convince himself that he slept. Edna kept her physically away in the evenings, but he dared not stay alone in the house.

He spent whole afternoons in the echoing coolness of the city museum where there was, among other things, a fully-equipped Romany caravan all baroque paintwork and engraved mirrors, with a stuffed tabby-cat curled on the steps; and a heavily decorated brass and scarlet fire engine; and also a great many skeletons. Best of all was the reassembled skeleton of an Irish elk on a landing. It was a huge and primeval beast and he looked at it endlessly, wishing he could somehow use it in a painting.

Sometimes, too, he would go to the reading room of the public library and read through all the day's papers, every scrap there was in them to read, including the sports pages, the strip cartoons, all the advertisements and the captions under every photograph. Around him was the stale smell of handled newspapers, of old age pensioners hung in bat-like clusters around and over the cool radiators as if to force some pale ghost of warmth from them to nourish their old bones. Five minutes after he left the library, he could never remember a single thing he had read.

In neither of these places was it likely that Ghislaine would come looking for him.

After a day thus divided between museum and library, he would make a furtive dash for home through the mellowing sunshine just as Edna, weary yet welcoming, put the final touches to their evening spaghetti or risotto, and he would lay before her, assembled in a sheaf of guilty flowers, the invented doings of a whole busy day.

Painting. Sometimes he wanted to paint, for he felt he would find a sort of peace in a total concentration on work with his hands, but he did not dare to go near his little workroom because it was over the shop and looked out on the dreary street, and Ghislaine, if she stood below and received no answer to her repeated drummings on the door where the white card with 'closed' on it swung, might raise her Medusa head and see him moving about behind the upper window.

He wanted to do things with his hands yet he could not summon up the energy to do the smallest physical task; for example to wash up the dishes from Edna's hurried and scanty breakfast in the mornings. The lipstick-stained spoon across the saucer in the cornflakes bowl would lie undisturbed under the cold tap as he hastily sluiced his face before scuttling out into the street and by the time Edna emptied it, much later, it had gathered a spilling pool of drips.

He had to pass the park on his way home, where a few late children tired themselves out before bedtime in a final, whirling game and the bright green grass was spotted as in a picture-book spring with clumps of precise daisies, looking as if butter wouldn't melt in their eyes. He averted his face as he went past, because it upset him to think that the merry children whooping and racing among the daisies would one day have to grow up, and cope with a brutal world.

One lunchtime, slipping unwisely into the Struldbrug café for a cup of tea, he saw a flash of gold and a whiplash of vermilion at a table in a corner. He turned at once and fled through the dangerous open air, retaining neither breath nor tranquillity until he had stood for long, peaceful minutes in the museum before the splendidly preserved 1904 brewer's dray, frozen in perpetuity in straining toil with two stuffed horses pulling it. His heart was thumping so painfully that he thought he might have a spectacular heart attack and he would be able to stay in bed legitimately, or, perhaps, even die.

When he recovered, he thought: 'Perhaps it was not she.' And slunk foolishly to the lavatory to steal a drink of water from the washbasin taps.

'You are a great coward,' he told his reflection in the cracked mirror of the bathroom he and his wife shared with a number of other tenants. He analyzed his reflection unhappily.

His Raskolnikov eyes, like dead coals, were altogether of too fine a cast – speaking too much blighted and heroic romanticism – for a poor shivering wretch such as himself. Mournfully, he tended to a ripe pimple on his upper lip, bending to the mirror to squeeze out the pus with two pinched fingers; he squeezed too hard and both blood and pus flowed upon his hand.

'I cannot make an adequate job, even, of squeezing a pimple.'

Upstairs, in the darkening evening, Edna industriously knitted a sweater for him, her hands darting like little white birds making nest. She would so much rather have been making small garments for their child but there was no child and no prospect of one, so she did the best she could.

Edna was by nature a nest builder, a home maker, a creator of warm cosiness, a real woman, a fine woman (no matter how flat

her breasts were); and what right had he, youngest, most ineffectual, weakest and most stupid of all the Brothers Karamazov
(so pathetically ineffectual that Dostoevsky could in the end find
no corner of the plot in which to fit him), what right had he to
batten on her compulsive urge to love?

Or, for that matter, what right had he to skulk in the bathroom when she got her knitting out because he could not bear
to sit like Dr Dale for three hours on end as she clicked domes-
tically away? When she had that very evening, over their meal
(instant curry from a dehydrated pack), congratulated herself on
having him so much at home these days, at home with her in a
cunning synthesis of cosiness?

'I shall get one of those kittens for her, indeed, I shall. It will
ease the strain.'

But the kitten would grow out of the fubsy, lovable stage and
become an arrogant and self-sufficient cat, gobbling her minced
liver and stalking away from her outstretched arms, sneering like
Oscar under its whiskers. It would make foul messes in the middle of the sanded floorboards and she would have to clear them up.

He remembered how he had sanded the floorboards for her, at
her request; it seemed to be the only task of love he had ever
performed for her, unless one included the actual wedding cer-
emony itself. He had sanded the floorboards all one November's
day, and she had been so pleased that he had privately promised
himself to paint the bedroom for her, before the spring came,
just to please her. But the brown flowerbunches still pocked the
paper on the bedroom walls. Love; a garland of wallpaper flowers on the grave of love.

His face in the mirror, his black beard and anguished features,
reminded him of Ghislaine's remark about the El Greco Christ.
But Ghislaine did not understand him or them or their relationship and its sorry logic. You can't waste love; only the most

reckless housewife throws it away. (Blood dripped down the upper part of his beard from the running pimple.) He thought (as he sopped up the blood with toilet paper) how Ghislaine might say that Edna crucified him with her knitting needles, if she saw them at home together, and then said aloud, shrugging (as he flushed the soiled paper down the lavatory), 'Oh, what a pathetic fool I am!' He tried to laugh at himself, against the swirling counterpoint of the running water.

But Ghislaine moved into his mind again, as promptly as if he had invited her, and installed herself there, bag and baggage. How fearful, yet how inevitable, it would be if, tonight, the charm refused to work and she rang his doorbell that very minute, as he sat in relative peace on the edge of the bath, narrow buttocks snug in the pile of the humorous bath mat they kept hanging there, out of the dirt. (Edna had bought the bath mat. It had two whimsical, black, naked footprints on a white ground and Morris found it hard to forgive her for liking such things.)

And Edna would innocently drag her slipper feet (daytime shoes off and on trees under the bed to preserve them better), drag slipper feet down three flights of aching stairs to open the door on that spectre, and it would say: 'Helloooo, Edna; I've come to sleep with Morris, Edna.'

He grew tense. A muscle in his neck started throbbing and his back grew stiff.

Time passed slowly. The collection of fraying toothbrushes on the ledge beside the lavatory wavered and grew indistinct as the light waned and he could no longer make out the gaudy lettering on the toothpaste packets. He moved once; he lifted a spider out of the bath and set it upon its feet on the floor, where it ran off under the door and away. He found he was almost crying when he thought of the poor spider, how it might have drowned if he had left it in the bath.

At the hour when he and Edna usually drank a cup of coffee before bed, he rose stiffly from his seat and went back to the living-room. She sat in the Pre-Raphaelite glow from the low, single lamp. Her brown hair she wore parted in the middle and smoothed sleekly over the nape of her neck and when she bent her head over the work in her lap, the curve of her brow and the lines of her shoulders and arms were harmonious, beautiful and predictable as a chord of music in a hymn.

She was a Victorian girl; a girl of the days when men were hard and top-hatted and masculine and ruthless and girls were gentle and meek and did a great deal of sewing and looked after the poor and laid their tender napes beneath a husband's booted foot, even if he brought home cabfuls of half-naked chorus girls and had them dance on the rich round mahogany dining-table (rosily reflecting great pearly hams and bums in its polished depths). Or, drunk to a frenzy, raped the kitchen-maid before the morning assembly of servants and children and her black silk-dressed self (gathered for prayers). Or forced her to stitch, on shirts, her fingers to rags to pay his gambling debts.

Husbands were a force of nature or an act of God; like an earthquake or the dreaded consumption, to be borne with, to be meekly acquiesced to, to be impregnated by as frequently as Nature would allow. It took the mindless persistence, the dogged imbecility of the grey tides, to love a husband.

Edna thought marriage was for submission and procreation. When she said, 'love, honour and obey' in the watered-milk light of the church where they had been married, her face glowed with such unearthly splendour that the brass pots on the altar holding a few late chrysanthemums were put to shame.

And when the parson reached the lines about 'procreation of children' she reached out, lambent, to touch his hand and turned eyes (softer than the white wool of babyclothes) to the ground, as if overwhelmed by the prospect of maternity.

Naturally, she resented contraception.

Not only did she think that it foiled the right, true end of love-making, which was making babies, but she constantly complained that she found the whole process undignified and disgusting. Her face puckered with disgust as she inserted the diaphragm. (It had taken six months of daily persuasion before she could master her shyness sufficiently to go to the Family Planning Clinic and get herself fitted with one in the first place; and then she had made him go with her, to give her courage, and stand waiting outside the gate for her and she had come out pale and trembling with the beginnings of tears in her eyes and silently showed him the package and wouldn't let him touch her for days.)

She always preferred to put it in in the kitchen, where he could not see her, although these preliminaries did not offend him in the least, rather giving him the security of knowing they had actually taken place. He was always afraid that after his customary denial when she asked him, 'Will you give me a baby, this time?' she would one day decide to take matters into her own hands. But if he insisted strongly enough, then he supposed she would be docile and obedient, because that was how wives should be.

He did not even persist in adultery, once she found him out in it; and thus again he failed her, through not being able to bear hurting her, for she would have found some satisfaction in having a persistently unfaithful husband, just as she would have found satisfaction in physical ill-treatment. It would at least show that he was *involved* with her, if he wished to betray or beat her. But he did not want to be involved with her; he wanted her to be happy without being involved in her happiness. So they lived in a ceaseless, never to be resolved dialectic.

Really, she wanted a good husband who would truly need her and dearly value her; but, failing that, a bad husband she could pride herself on loving all the same was her heart's desire. Morris fell painfully between two stools. Once, and once only, had he tried to be a wicked husband; the time he had half-heartedly attempted to steer her into bed with Oscar, who was attracted by her gentle moth-colourings, the browns and greys and beiges of her, by virtue of the contrast with the crude primaries of his own personality.

Nightly pillows were soaked with tears after, aghast, she bundled a baffled Oscar from the flat as he fumbled with his fly and demanded: 'Why? Why?' His approach had indeed been unmistakably direct and she thought he was a horrid animal. For a long time she wondered if she 'ought to tell' Oscar's wife, with whom she occasionally made jam when fruit was cheap in the early autumn and for whose babies she had made matinée jackets and bootees, mournfully and enviously and lovingly. Yet it was not Oscar whom she blamed and eventually she had decided it would be best for all of them to keep the attack secret, since Oscar had been overruled by passion and was not quite himself, surely, at the time. She blamed herself; she must, somehow, have tempted him. The long and painful crawl she made back to self-esteem after she had decided she had tempted Oscar had brought Morris down terribly.

Yet now, in the soft light, she looked so tender and homely as she sat with her knitting that Morris felt an odd desire for her sort of tenderness and homeliness. He wanted, for a moment, to scoop her on to his knee and bury his face in the yielding cushion of her chignon, murmuring: 'My little comfort,' in the way that the sort of husband she wanted might have done when they still wore collars stapled to their shirts with disks of mother-o'-pearl. He was so heavy with misery that he wanted to pull Edna's fluffy muffler of love warmly around him. He stood in the doorway, biting his nails. She spoke first.

'It was a very long bath that you just had, darling.'

He remembered with a start that he had told her he was going to have a bath when he fled to the bathroom and lied fluently. 'The water ran cold half-way through and I had to wait for more. Someone must be doing washing somewhere.'

To himself, his voice sounded pale and shivering, and to her, also; she glanced up at him quizzically and something snapped inside him. He broke out in a long wail.

'Oh, please, please – put down your knitting!'

She made brown question-marks of her eye-brows and obediently laid the work aside. She was making him a big, black sweater which he would accept ungraciously and wear to smelly rags without a word of thanks. She had reached the point in its making where soon she would wish to hold the panel up, measuring it against his body to see how it would look, as you hold a picture speculatively against a wall; he always found this peculiarly humiliating.

'Something terrible has happened,' he said. He could contain it no longer. 'You will have to know it. Ghislaine is back.'

There was a long pause.

'I see.' The sibilant rustled, like a small, silk undergarment, the petticoat of some dwarf. He was still in sufficient control of himself to be irritated with her for answering him with this commonplace when it was impossible that she should see the implications for them both of what he had said, before he told her what effect Ghislaine's return had had on him.

'She was in the pub, that night, when you had a headache,' he said, so that she would not think he had visited Ghislaine when she was in hospital. Edna pretended she was counting stitches so that she would not have to look at him.

'Why did you not tell me at once, Morris?'

'I love my love with an M,' thought Morris grimly, 'because his name is Morris and he is monstrous.'

'Because I thought it might upset you,' he said out loud. 'I didn't want to upset you, Edna, dearest.' Just in time, he remembered to tag on the endearment.

Her eyes still down, she said in a low voice: 'And do you still feel the same way about her?' She caught her breath, almost sobbed: 'Is that what you want to tell me?'

He could have burst into tears himself, because she did not understand.

'Edie, she is dreadful, dreadful, she is repulsive –'

'How cruel, to say such a thing!'

'Ah, you should see her! She looks like –'

'But, surely, all that would stop you telling me about her would be that you wanted her again and –'

Her hands twitched, her face worked in an agony of non-comprehension. He felt hysteria rising but managed valiantly to control it. He spoke coolly, calmly, appeasingly.

'Please, Edna, dearest, I said I was sorry at the time, and I meant it. And I'm still more sorry than I can say. But she has this scar all down her face now and it is nothing to do with wanting her or not wanting her, but it is so dreadful, this scar, when she was such a lovely girl, before. And never again. Try – try and think how it must be for her. And I have been feeling badly about it.'

He swayed from the door and slumped down on a chair, for he was not strong enough to continue standing any longer. He caught sight of the history of the French Second Empire; its covers glowed red in the light of the lamp and he looked away hurriedly, upset, and stared at Edna as, obediently, she tried to imagine how Ghislaine must be suffering.

Slowly, a change came over her features. She clasped her hands before her. Just as, seeing she was softening, he was about to taste the enormous relief of telling her of his guilt, she cried out: 'Oh, the poor, poor thing!' and the force of her compassion for the other woman silenced him.

Her grey eyes widened with compassion, her narrow mouth trembled with compassion and the sweater fell disregarded to the floor. 'Compassion', Millais would have called her, with her upturned face and incandescent eyes and long hands joined like the ears of a butchered rabbit. In a pompous gilt frame, she would have been exhibited at the Royal Academy and afterwards reproduced in the *Illustrated London News*, to subsequently grace a thousand humble walls up and down the country. She was so full of compassion for Ghislaine that she would think he was being merely childishly selfish if he now ventured to talk of himself.

'Morris, I must ask you – about Honey. Is it true what they say – about him and her and what he did to her?'

He could not but tell her the truth; she was his wife. He said, 'Yes,' in a subdued, colourless voice. His teeth, he realized, had begun to ache, all together, in concert; all the canines and molars sang in chorus. It was the last straw. He wished he were dead.

'Yes,' he repeated, sucking his teeth. Why was she going on and on and on?

'How could he have done such a thing!'

He burst out in sudden irritation because his teeth were aching and she was so censorious and morally indignant and compassionate and did not see how unhappy he was.

'Edna, you ought to know how someone could want to hurt Ghislaine! Don't you remember how you said you wanted to kill her when –'

'That's unfair!' As indeed, it was. By accusing her of jealous fury, he lowered himself in her eyes. He was checkmated again.

'I think she is wandering a little in her mind,' he told her, to draw her mind from the uneasy past to the uneasy present. 'She is going looking for Honey everywhere. I think I catch glimpses of her everywhere I go; I've got to thinking that she is looking for me. I run away when I see her.'

He prayed that Edna might see from his halting statement something of what he was undergoing.

'Why do you run away from her, Morris? Do you feel she still has a hold over you?'

'I am frightened,' he said simply. 'I have been afraid she might come here for me.' Oh, please understand, he said wordlessly, please understand.

'Oh, Morris.' Reproachfully. What was she thinking, inside her impregnable head under the bulging chignon?

'I don't want you to be upset, Edie.'

'Upset?' she exclaimed.

'You see,' he said, walking restlessly about the room, 'she asked me to bring her back here.' He was still throbbing with toothache.

And they were further apart than ever and she grew more and more uncomprehending every moment; he saw that with every word he said he went further and further down in her estimation, down, down, down, because he was being selfish and unfeeling about the poor, scarred girl.

'But where is she living? Has she nowhere to go?'

'No, no, Edna, it's not that. She just wanted to get some confirmation that she could still have a man if she tried.'

She brushed him aside.

'Where is she living?'

'I don't know.'

'Didn't you even find out if she had anywhere proper to sleep? A sick girl?'

'She used to have a little room. Why shouldn't she still have her little room? She hasn't been away such a time.'

A spectrum of emotions flashed across her face so swiftly that Morris was unable to isolate individual emotions and gained only a generalized impression of emotional strife at furious brew behind the smooth, white china forehead. Outside, the pussy-cat face of the moon hung in the sky as if balanced on an invisible jet of water, like the ping-pong balls at shooting ranges.

'How lucky the moon is, all up there and cool,' he thought. He looked out of the window, enviously, at the moon.

'She must come here,' Edna said.

He lowered his face on to the cool pane. It was too much. What further astonishing rabbit might she produce from her hat?

'No, Edie.'

'Yes,' she said inexorably, for the broken tones of his voice had no fierce command in them to deter her. 'Yes. We are all human beings and we must love one another. I shall try to look after her, even though she hurt me so. That is what Christians call charity.'

'Bloody Christians,' thought Morris. He rubbed his forehead over and over the windowpane, smearing it with sweat. His teeth ached so much he thought his head might blow up. He hoped his head would explode like a roman candle and leave Edna gazing open-mouthed at his lifeless body, a charred stump for a neck.

'Edna,' he began, 'I am so afraid of her –' But she cut him short.

'How can you be so cruel about her when you had – what you had – with her. You are so heartless that it grieves me. How can you –'

'A little bit of sex, *that* was all I had with her. And precious little it was, too. You soon put a stop to that, didn't you, screaming and shouting and talking about trust and faith and love and how you'd lay down your life for me, you bitch!'

'Oh, don't be so horrible to me!'

'I'm not having that woman in my house and that's flat!' He was becoming excited and his voice rose. He crashed his fist against the window pane and all the glass rattled. The slow tears formed, fell down her face. Miraculously he had taken the right line with her, the strong line.

The atmosphere between them electrified. Their eyes caught and held. His aching teeth gave a final excruciating chord and modulated to a gentle pianissimo that hardly troubled him. She looked very small and defenceless and her tear-darkened eyes had love, love, love in them. He found he wanted to make love to her.

'Is it just because she is crying? Do I only want her because I have made her cry?' he wondered, rather shocked at himself, even while he moved across the room to her. He kicked aside the knitting which caught at his feet as if it were a little black dog, trying to protect its mistress from him.

4

The lilacs were all withered and women walked with bare and honey-coloured shoulders and the little children who did nothing but play in the sun all day were the colour of the Red Indians they imagined themselves to be and the round trees lumbered in the little winds, all top-heavy with shifting leaves, and the dust curded thickly on the heaped junk in his shop before Honeybuzzard returned. Morris hung motionless in the spring like a fly in a spiderweb, paralyzed.

One morning, as, after a first quick reconnaisance, Morris sat drinking a first cup of coffee in the cafe, slinking in a corner, he saw a young girl enter. She stood peering uncertainly around her, screwing up myopic eyes. Morris had never seen her before and she seemed a stranger; her appearance was not quite that of the girls of the city and he thought: 'London. Or, maybe, Liverpool.' Her hair was chopped off in a fringe above lightly marked eyebrows and curled in dark commas into her cheeks below the ears. There was a dolly patch of bright pink in the centre of each round cheek. An easy skirt of blue denim ended above her knees and her legs were unusually thin and elegant. She wore a red and white striped sweater and her breasts were exceptionally round, large and high. She wore bright white knee socks and a pair of two-tone, lace-up, low-heeled shoes in red and green. From her shoulder hung a duffel bag starred with a pennant, 'Southend'. Her face was calm, blank but serious, with a strong, broad jaw and in her arms she carried a very white cat. Morris had never seen a girl carrying a cat in the café before.

The cat lay somnolent, as if drugged, and she carried it like a baby in the crook of her arms; but not like a baby, for she carried it not affectionately but casually, as though it might have been a bundle of washing cradled in her arms because, that way, it was easier to carry. Morris supposed that the girl and her cat were waiting for someone; but who could they belong to?

They belonged to Honeybuzzard.

Who came in pat, like the catastrophe in an old comedy. Honeybuzzard, lithe and slick as a stick of liquorice in his black leather jacket and corduroy trousers. Honeybuzzard, who seemed to be affecting a Groucho Marx stunt walk, his black legs scuttling in the wake of his thrust-forward torso. Honeybuzzard, crowned with an extremely large peaked cap, checked in screaming orange and shouting purple, pulled well down over his forehead and a mass of blond hair tumbling to his shoulders in a faint drift of dandruff. He had on a new pair of owl-round, emphatically black sunglasses. He looked like a Hollywood starlet unsuccessfully attempting incognito.

Morris had never fully accustomed himself to the shock that Honey's flamboyant and ambiguous beauty gave him each time he saw him again after an absence. In the midst of his relief at seeing Honey, Mr Fixit himself, home once more, he even now found he had to check a desire to wolf-whistle in derisive admiration. He eclipsed the girl with the cat even though she was a little taller than he; he eclipsed her literally and figuratively, as he scooped her up into his black leather arms, there in the middle of the café, and thrust his face into her neck. He clung to her for a long minute and then pushed her away and gazed about the room, grinning.

Honeybuzzard had the soft, squashy-nosed, full-lipped face one associates with angels blowing glad, delirious trumpets in early Florentine pictures of the Nativity; a nectarine face, bruisable and somehow juicy, covered with a close, golden fuzz that thickened into a soft, furry, animal down on his jaw but never actually coalesced into a beard (he had never, in all his life, needed to shave). He had a pair of perfectly pointed ears, such as fauns have and, curiously, these were also covered with down; his pointed ears poked whimsically through his golden lovelocks, under the shadow of the extraordinary cap. And then, disquieting, strange, at odds with the cherub-face, there was the mouth.

It was impossible to look at the full, rich lines of his dark red mouth without thinking: 'This man eats meat.' It was an inexpressibly carniverous mouth; a mouth that suggested snapping, tearing, biting, a mouth that was always half-smiling in a pretty, feline curve; and showing in the smile, hints of feline, tearing teeth, small, brilliantly white, sharp, like wounding little chips of milk glass. How beautiful he was, and how indefinably sinister.

The black beam from the dark glasses hit Morris squarely and at once Honey threw his arms open in a great theatrical gesture of greeting and came leaping towards him with a great whoop of 'Morris, darling!' Early coffee businessmen rustled disapproving newspapers but the girl did not seem to be at all disconcerted. Light shot off Honey's shiny leather jacket in fusillades; he seemed to snap and crackle as he moved. He hugged Morris warmly and put his wet, long mouth against Morris's forehead in a token kiss of greeting. He was pulsing with suppressed laughter.

'Christ, it's a rich life!' he said, collapsing giggling on the chair beside Morris. The girl followed him decorously. He watched her walk steadily, one foot before the other, shaking his head as if he did not believe in her. Morris was nonplussed by the presence of the girl.

'Meet my lovely Emily, Morris,' said Honey, taking Morris's hand and putting it on the girl's as soon as she came near enough. Her hand was half-buried in her cat's coat; Morris had a mingled sensation of hard flesh and soft fur.

'This is lovely Emily, which is her given-gingham-bloody-apron name, ain't it a gas? Emily, this is Morris, David to my Jonathan. I think.'

'Pleased to meet you.' South London vowels, long and flat, like a file of dignified dachshunds, and a grave movement of the lips that had little to do with the action of smiling and seemed to indicate that she was not in the least pleased to see him at all but was accustomed to taking part in such silly word games although she inwardly despised them. Morris could not understand why Honeybuzzard was so ebullient, the girl so calm. 'What is going on?' he thought.

'Put the cat down, Emily, and take a seat,' said Honeybuzzard, growing more composed.

She obediently set the cat down on the table and seated herself, crossing her legs with a scissory sound of rasping nylon. Morris saw she was wearing stockings underneath the white knee socks and this puzzled him. The cat lay stiffly half on and half off the table; it lay where she placed it, stark, making no attempt to curl itself up and be comfortable, after the manner of cats. Morris thought it might be dead.

'Your cat – is it quite well?'

'I gave it an aspirin for the journey, because they get excited, cats, travelling, see. An aspirin is a real knock-out drop to a cat.'

'I see,' said Morris.

She made her symbol of a smile again. Her lips were fat, pink and unpainted. Then she bent her head to inspect her fingernails, which were enamelled silver. Her glossy black hair swung down across her carnation cheeks. It was obvious she did not wish to speak any more, just then, if at all. She sat on her chair with a stone-like stolidity, as if she had sat down once and for all. It was impossible to imagine her ever getting up and walking again. Morris thought how clean her fingernails were.

'I thought,' said Honeybuzzard, 'that it would be nice if Emily could help in the shop.' She did not look up. Her fingernails absorbed her.

'I am sure,' said Morris incredulously, 'that she would be a great help.'

Honeybuzzard slithered a quick, black glance at him, 'Are things not going well, then? You sound satirical. You ought to be welcoming me home, with jingling pocketfuls of profits for me.'

'I haven't been near the shop since you went away.' The presence of the girl disconcerted and offended Morris. How could he talk freely about Ghislaine in front of the girl. He lowered his voice. 'Would the young lady like to go to the powder room?'

Honeybuzzard raised his eyebrows so far they shot up above the rims of the black glasses but said: 'Emily, be a love and go to the lavatory for five minutes, please.'

She rose at once. It was a conjuring trick. 'Take care of my cat,' she said. She walked through the cafe looking neither to right nor left and Honeybuzzard smugly watched the even dip of her brief skirt.

'My Emily,' he said cheerfully. 'Rich, moist and sticky. Fruitcake. My Emily is like nothing so much as the very best fruitcake, the kind with rum in it that you can get drunk on. I gorge on her, like a baby at a party. Oh, my, oh, my.'

'For Chrissake listen, Honey – Ghislaine has left the hospital. She's looking for you.'

There was a silence. The bright face under the bright cap was a mask of nothing. Morris became aware of the ticking of a large clock inset above his head into the wall. A fly buzzed around his head.

'Oh?' said Honey at last. 'And has anything else happened?'

'My God, aren't you going to do anything about her?'

'Why should I do anything? And what can I do that the National Health Service can't do better?'

'Honey –' cried Morris, in pain.

'Please be quiet, Morris,' said the mask authoritatively. 'Let's go to the shop, soon; I want to see how its been looking after itself, since you left the sinking ship, you rat.'

'And what then?'

'Emily will make us some delicious lunch. She cooks quite well, though one tends to get a lot of tinned beans.' The mask giggled again, remembering something private.

'Oh, Honey, I've been ill with worry since you were away.'

'You just can't get along without me, can you, darling

Morris opened his mouth, then shrugged and subsided. There was a pause. Then Honeybuzzard asked, almost slyly: 'Is she very ugly, though, now?'

'She's very frightening.'

'These teenagers, so violent, so vicious – they should be horsewhipped. Fancy doing that to a poor young girl!'

Bewildered, Morris tried to see the eyes under the sunglasses but only saw his own face blackly reflected. Was Honey really believing his own stories? Had he decided to believe the lie, as he had done before with other lies? But he could not tell. He could only tell that Honey had decided on his story and was sticking to it, even with him.

'She is very frightening,' he repeated. 'She would frighten your shiny new Emily.'

'Then she mustn't meet my Emily, must she? But very little frightens my Emily. We were having it off on the settee in her Tooting front room in the blue television gloaming and her drunken father came raging in with a breadknife and a mouthful of threats; she simply put a clean pair of knickers in her bag and picked up her cat and walked out.'

'She's fond of the cat, then?'

'So it would seem.'

Honey was probably lying again; but his tale appealed to Morris. He pictured the scene in his mind's eye, white flesh on uncut moquette and the operatic entrance of the enraged father.

'And you were quite unruffled, while this happened, were you?'

'I was ruffled as a turkey cock, man. I went through the window, which happened to be open, thank God. It was like a Whitehall farce, only with sex – life imitates art, you know, I always thought it did. Like an arrow from a bow, through the window I went as soon as I saw him, the great peasant brute. I never had a chance to do up my trousers till I reached Tooting Broadway tube station. Never been so embarrassed, darling.'

He made a mincing gesture with his right hand and tittered. There was a Renaissance poison ring on his right hand. He said there was curare in it, and he could put death in his handshake, if he wanted to; but Morris had never believed him. He suspended belief in the Tooting Broadway incident, too, and came back, wincing, to the café.

'How can you be so calm.'

'She's nothing to do with me any more, darling.'

'But she is sure to come to the shop for you –'

'I don't care. Let her go, let her go!' He flung Ghislaine to the winds, with the gesture of the sower in the parable. Fascinated, Morris watched her blow away. Honeybuzzard put a comforting arm around his shoulders. 'And never you fret, Morris, I'll look after you.' Morris wished he could be sure of it.

'Now change the subject,' commanded Honeybuzzard. So Morris changed the subject.

'I went to the sale. I bought some stuffed birds. They cost twenty-five shillings.'

'Very good, when one considers the price stuffed birds are fetching now.'

'But the glass case is all broken and the birds themselves seem to have caught a sort of bird eczema.'

'Oh.'

Morris was still unhappy and could not control it. He moaned, dismissing the stuffed birds: 'But she will be everywhere, still!'

'Oh, no, she won't. Now be quiet about Ghislaine. She's beginning to bore me.' The voice was so sharp that Morris started. But Honeybuzzard was now gently pulling the cat from the table on to his lap and his movements were as kind as bread and honey. Honey.

'I'm going to hide Emily's cat in case the management thinks it's unhygienic.' He tucked the unprotesting cat away inside his jacket as the singing Struldbrug rushed up and slid her rag immediately across the table. She screwed up one eye, obscenely; Nelson.

'Turned a blind eye, I did! Tee, hee, no cats allowed on tables. But I turned a blind eye for my sweetheart. Two sweethearts?' she added interrogatively. Honeybuzzard smiled at her and she smiled gladly back.

'That was nice of you,' said Morris. 'Thank you.'

'Nice to be appreciated, eh, darling? eh?'

'Yes,' he said. She sidled away, huddled in her grey overall under the great, bowed fatness of her shoulders.

'Funny old woman.' Honeybuzzard took his tobacco and his interesting black cigarette papers to industriously roll himself a cigarette. 'How's Edna ? She wasn't too good when I saw her last.'

'She's all right. But she wants Ghislaine to come and live with us. She wants to look after Ghislaine, because that's what Christians call charity.'

'Well, isn't that nice; what a lovely thought.' He licked his cigarette and stuck it together. 'I don't know how you can live with that woman, Morris. Some women you can only vivisect and she's one of them, the pink-eyed, laboratory-rat sort of woman.

'Here's a man who tried to vivisect her, but he found only knitting needles and porridge and pilches,' he continued, for Oscar was coming towards them with his cup of tea and an expression of restrained gladness on his face. Honey lit the cigarette, and waved invitingly to Oscar with it.

'You're a very fortunate man,' said Oscar, seating himself at the table and clumsily arranging the bulky parcels of his great limbs. 'You've got back at the right time.'

'Oh ? Why's that?'

'She has gone back to hospital.'

'Who, Ghislaine?' broke in Morris. 'But –'

'How could you know, Morris; you've been hiding yourself away. It is a long story and not a very pleasant one. She appeared at Henry Glass's flat, one night. You remember she lived with Henry Glass for a few weeks?'

Henry Glass was a small, spotted, quiet man, gentle as a house-trained Dalmatian, who made jewellery in an insanitary basement. Briefly ignited by Ghislaine's bonfire, he flared with her for a single manic month and, after her departure, relapsed into an unlikely marriage with a Finnish *au pair* girl, whose command of the English language was limited to perhaps fifty basic words and a single, all-embracing tense. They were, curiously, very happy. She, now hugely pregnant, a soft-eyed, wide-hipped, cow-woman, prepared lavish meals for him and even in the slumbrous dream in which she moved, managed to keep his basement extravagantly clean. Henry Glass had grown fat and content. His acne cleared up. His drains stopped smelling. His underwear, once unguessable, now weekly on public display at the launderette, was neatly patched and darned.

'Henry Glass woke up to find Ghislaine coming knocking at his door three nights ago, asking to be let in. But he wouldn't, because of his wife, for he doesn't know enough Finnish to be able to explain about it to her and, anyway, Ghislaine was drunk.'

'Drunk? I've never seen her drunk,' said Morris, astonished.

'Things have changed. She was very drunk. So she got very angry and upset and took earth from a windowbox –'

'He's got window-boxes, now, has he?' inquired Honeybuzzard, with detached, amused interest. He was playing it all very cool.

'He's got window boxes, yes –'

'What does he grow in them?'

Oscar took off his half-smile. He was obviously beginning to be irritated. 'Geraniums,' he said. 'And white alyssum, and he's got some pots of herbs for his wife's cooking.'

'How nice. Do go on.' Honeybuzzard blew a round and perfect smoke-ring which hovered and dissolved above his head like an emanation. They all watched it, even Oscar; it seemed a numinous and portentous thing. Then Oscar set his teeth and went on.

'Ghislaine took earth from these window-boxes and rubbed handfuls of it in her face, tearing open the scar and rubbing the earth into the open wound. And then she rushed away, screaming. Now she is back in hospital, very ill with blood poisoning. Henry Glass in under sedation — nerves — and his wife almost miscarried with the shock.'

Morris took the makings of a cigarette from Honeybuzzard and busied himself with the loose, moist tobacco; he wanted something to do with his hands and he did not want to be forced to look at Oscar. His hands shook and scattered grains of tobacco on the table. His mouth was dry and his head swam. He could not take all that Oscar had said in. Honey said nothing but blew a number of smoke-rings and put his finger through one of them before it vanished. Oscar noisily drank his forgotten tea, and pushed the empty cup away.

'She doesn't seem to be asking after you, Honey,' he said.

'And why should she? I am just a friend.'

'Why should she, indeed? Still, I thought you would like to hear the news. After you've been away so long.'

'Oh, yes, I like to hear what's been going on.' Amiable and affable, cradling the cat, distanced and detached, Honeybuzzard suddenly clapped his hand to his pocket. 'I've brought back something from London, something to make you laugh, Oscar. . . .'

He now produced a small, plastic rose on a coiling rubber stem attached to a bulb and slipped it into his buttonhole. Manoeuvring the lapel towards Oscar's face, he pressed the hidden bulb and an obscene, ridged, pink, tactile, rubber worm leaped out, quivered momentarily, and then sank back into the crimson nest of plastic petals, detumescent.

'I got it from a joke-shop outside the British Museum,' he said. 'It was only sixpence. It was ever such a bargain, I think. Isn't it a scream? Isn't it a scream?' he insisted, leaning over the table and jerking the horrid thing again and again in Oscar's face.

Oscar, nonplussed, gaped. Then, deliberately, Honey took off his gaudy cap and set it back to front on Oscar's head, pealing with laughter. Oscar came back to life and angrily flung the cap to the ground.

'Are you trying to make a fool of me?' he asked dangerously.

'If you hadn't moved, I would have put false ears and vampire teeth on you and sent you through the streets with a label on your back, "kick me",' said Honey through his laughter. 'You're a fool already but let's tell the world!'

He picked up his cap and dusted it, tugged Morris by the hand and left Oscar alone, simmering to himself.

'Fat bastard, fat bastard, fat bastard,' murmured Honey over and over again beneath his breath, in a sort of litany. All laughter was gone, as if wiped away with a cloth. Morris dazedly went with him; he was thinking about Ghislaine.

'I should have taken her home. I should. It was my duty.' He should have bedded her snugly on the long wicker-chair, tucking blankets round her and feeding her hot milk and dripping toast and egg custard and given her warmth and security and spared her the frenzy of rejection and despair. He promised himself he would go to see her, under her mound of bandages, in the white metal bed, and urge her to come and live with Edna and himself, that they would love her and care for her and ask nothing of her and nobody would harm her again, never again.

Yet he knew all the time that he would never carry out so much of this resolution as to actually get to the hospital and find his way to her ward, and that it was only the knowledge that she was somewhere safe where she could not speak to him or show herself to him or affect him in any way that enabled him to pity her from his entire heart.

Emily was coaxing a packet of raisins and nuts from a machine by the door.

'You were all talking to that great fat man. I didn't like his face so I stayed out here.'

'That's a good girl,' Honeybuzzard approved, patting her blue denim buttocks. She cuddled at her cat again. It opened its eyes, slowly, so that the inside eyelid, whitey-pink, formed a half-open shutter across the pupil, and yawned out a tiny, uncertain mew. Then its eyes closed again.

'How old is your cat?' asked Morris, to distract himself.

'About two.'

'Isn't it very big, though, for two years old?'

'It's full grown. It's not very big reely.'

'I was thinking of buying my wife a kitten. She likes looking after things.'

'Cats don't thank you for looking after them.'

'Oh.' The distraction was ineffectual.

With her height and her strong face and her heavy tread, one might almost have taken her for a boy dressed up as a girl in the

Elizabethan theatre, when transvestisism was an art form; what a foil she made for Honey's golden softness. They made a confusing and picturesque couple, embracing (again). But Morris saw superimposed on both their features the other face, the scarred face, set in a hieratic mask of grief.

5

Inside the shop, the dirty windows strained sunlight into a thick, rich puree, so that one had the sensation of swimming in soup. There was no window to open, no ventilation of any kind, and the thick, sour smell of dirt and neglect hung always in the solidified air, a sort of sub-aqueous, deep-sea atmosphere in which piles of furniture and rags and tea-chests seemed the encrusted, drowned cargoes of long-dead ships. There should have been limpets and seaweed on them. An antique gramophone advanced its ribbed, red horn towards Emily's white ankles, grabbing at her as if to swallow her into its mysterious, sea-anenome bowels while she intrepidly marched through a sea-bottom filled with hidden peril. Her bag knocked a heap of gramophone records from the glass case of a large stuffed badger; many of them broke. She did not apologize.

Honeybuzzard invited her to sit upon an Abbotsford oak chair, all wooden curlicues and snarling lions and martial but non-heraldic coats of arms, and a heap of calf-bound, late eighteenth-century sermons slithered out from under her as she did so.

Honey pulled off his jacket, revealing a new, very white, very frilly shirt with sleeves as wide as swan's wings. He slung his jacket around the pocked shoulders of a green-stained statue from some abandoned garden, now probably a housing estate or petrol station.

It was the statue of a broken, naked boy with a fierce dog beside him, reaching up with bared teeth eagerly, perhaps to snap off his genitals. The boy already wore a brocaded hat, part of the dress uniform of an Edwardian military gentleman. Honey had taken for himself the military gentleman's tall, high-heeled boots. The boy also wore a false nose. There was a red litter of false noses everywhere and Honey picked one up at random and put it on. At the foot of the garden boy five black and gold tins, each with an elaborate and incomprehensible Chinese character on its belly, congregated mutely. Behind his head, pinned on the wall, was a black kimono with many coupling dragons embroidered on the cracking silk.

And that was one corner of the shop only.

'You've got a lot of stuff, here,' Emily said calmly, and began to nibble her nuts and raisins. The smooth, scarcely inflected flow of her speech gave the merest remark the stature of an official pronouncement; she might have been announcing that the Queen had a slight chill and was confined to her room.

'Well, the early summer isn't a very busy time. We get a lot, well, not a lot, but some tourists later on. And we've got a lot of left-over stock on our hands at the moment. Not that it's a very good place for an antique shop, though.' Morris floundered among excuses. He was unhappily convinced of an obligation to tell the girl that the unseemly chaos around her was the norm, so that she was prepared from the very beginning for the worst. But, unconcerned, she ate a raisin and spat out the pip.

Outside, in the somnolent heat, a child in drooping shorts and filthy tee-shirt, its face hidden by a mask of jam and chocolate, poked a long stick down a foul drain. Nothing else moved. Morris, stifling, opened the door and a whiff of rotting meat from the butcher's next door punched him in the stomach. On the other side of their shop, a tobacconist and confectioner's inched towards bankruptcy. He was slowly dying of cancer in the curtained room beside the yellowing display of newspapers and stale cigarettes, and his wife, white as new bread, limply attended the infrequent customer, while in the glass jars the pear-drops slowly congealed to a glaucous mass and the extra-strong peppermints dissolved to aromatic dust.

Across the road, where a discarded newspaper raised up one broken wing, the great façade, tall chimneys and continually buzzing machines of a large laundry indicated, by its size and prosperity, the astounding dirtiness of the world.

'That child ought to be at school,' observed Honeybuzzard. 'I wonder why it isn't. Perhaps it has got an infectious disease.'

The only sound in the shop was the faint crunch of Emily's teeth on a nut. Then the cat jumped from her knee and stretched itself, shooting out each leg to a prodigious length. Slowly, wobbling a little, still partially drugged, it cuffed idly in dreamy slow motion at a ragged fringe of peacock feathers in an art nouveau pot.

'What is the name of your cat?' Morris asked her courteously.

'Tom,' she said.

'Why is that?'

'Because he's all male'.

'But doesn't it ejaculate around the house? Isn't that inconvenient?'

'It can do what it likes. You don't castrate somebody just because it makes it more convenient for yourself, do you?

The pink mouth snapped firmly shut. Morris felt chastened.

Then Emily did a surprising thing; she kicked off her two-tone shoes without undoing the laces and pulled off her long, white sock and her long, brown stockings, and drawing towards her at the same time, with the other foot, a little, humpy footstool some elderly Victorian virgin had once decorated with a petit-point picture of a rustic cottage and a peasant with a sheep-crook (both now badly damaged by moth). Then the girl took a tiny bottle out of her duffel bag, propped one foot on the other on the footstool and began to paint her toenails silver. Her unruffled calm and the sense of premeditated purpose in her movements surprised Morris. He hovered beside her, wishing he could think of something to say.

First she painted her great toenail and waggled it in the air, observing the effect. She seemed to have prehensile toes. Then, nodding approval to herself, she continued till all the toes on that foot were silver. Then she stripped off the other shoe, sock and stocking and started work on the other foot. Honeybuzzard, as if stimulated into activity by the girl's concentration on the job in hand, improvised a duster and moved about the shop flicking away at everything in a little cloud.

He sang to himself:

'Rock, rock me, baby, roll me in your great big chair,
'Rock and roll me, baby, till I can't tell which from where. . . .'

Emily raised her head, turning her eyes, which were blue, towards the opaque pools of Honey's dark glasses. The song died away. It was a private moment. Morris went out to the shed at the back where the lavatory was and relieved himself, in order to leave them alone together.

In the yard, the sunlight fell on his head as if emptied from a sack. He turned his face up to the sun for a few minutes to take it like medicine. The dandelions in a crack in the back wall had turned from suns to moons since he had seen them last. He picked one and blew away the spores, one, two, three; they hung airily around him in the windless stillness. 'Three o'clock and time for tea.' No doubt Emily would make them a cup of tea. He was sure, for some reason, that Emily would make very good tea.

Honeybuzzard, cap right at very tip of streetboy back of head, came into the yard as he absently stood with the bald dandelion in his hand, flipped it away and placed there, instead, a letter. The letter must have been poked through their letter slit some time ago, for it was dusty, and now marked heavily with their three incoming sets of footprints as it had lain unnoticed on the doormat. The letter contained three lines of self-abasing scribble, forgiving Honeybuzzard enormously and giving an address. The signature was a histrionic and unreadable flourish on top of which, perched like a little tricorne, one could make out a circumflex. She always put the circumflex in 'Ghîslaine'. Morris dropped the letter; it stung him.

He was about to speak when Honey laid a warning finger to his lips. From a window directly above them that Morris could never recall having been opened before came the clink of crockery and the gurgle of water. Emily was obviously already busy in the primitive little upstairs kitchen. The finger trembled; Honey was shaking with laughter. Today, he was always laughing. Then he took out his large and ostentatious gold cigarette lighter and lit the letter. In the strong sunlight, the flame was pale and ineffectual-looking; it hardly looked capable of burning the piece of paper but, magically, the paper blackened and crumbled. Hardly knowing why, Morris caught at a charred fragment floating in the air; when he unclenched his fingers, all that remained was a long, dark smear of soot across his palm.

'She's coming back crawling to me!' whispered Honey. 'Oh, my God, ain't it a gas? What do you make of that! I could marry her for that, almost – but she's going to have to crawl much farther than that for me, first; she'll have to crawl till her knees are all bloody, poor little girl!'

He reeled and hiccupped, spinning round the yard, bouncing against the wall, throwing his cap into the air and catching it. Morris ran his tongue around his teeth; they were aching again. Perhaps it was psychosomatic. He found he wanted to go home.

He would go home, get away from Honeybuzzard, soon; he would buy a box of chocolates for Edna from the distressed sweetshop next door and he would spend a quiet evening with Edna and be as nice as he could to her and allow her to drape him with her knitting and perhaps he would ring up the hospital to see how Ghislaine was, if Edna thought that he should. And he would stay away from the shop, in future; he would not see so much of Honey, in future. It was all getting too difficult. He turned away.

Honey took hold of both his shoulders and gripped him fast.

'Morris, don't go! Why are you going? Where are you going? I thought we would go out together, tonight. Have you been out since I've been in London?'

'No,' said Morris doubtfully. But he did not try to get away, although he knew that he ought to.

'Morris, as we were coming into town I saw some houses that have just been emptied. Around William Square. Old houses; and they've only just been turned out of them, the tenants. I shouldn't think anyone has been there, yet. Shall we go there, tonight, and see what we can find?'

Morris hesitated, sniffing at the bait, at first reluctant – then increasingly tempted.

'They're interesting houses, aren't they,' he said. 'Old and big, the houses in William Square.'

'Very empty and very big and very, very old.'

Morris licked his dry lips. 'It is such a long time since we were out together last. I've missed it.' An addict, he reached cautious, desiring hands to the syringe after a long period of abstinence.

Honey, his fish hooked, sighed, perhaps with relief, and took off his dark glasses to clean them. He only unmasked himself in this way when he was feeling particularly sure of himself, for he did not like to expose his eyes. His eyes were large and pale, with long, fair lashes; huge eyes, that blinked and stuttered in the light like shy children. His delicate, pick-pocket hands dealt gracefully with his glasses; such pretty, pink-and-white butter-fly hands. But they were extraordinarily, deceptively strong; Morris had once seen him tear a telephone directory in half with his pretty hands. They were dirty, though, and there was a hint of something rusty in the fingernails, rusty like dried blood.

Emily called: 'There's tea, if you want.'

'You need a cup of tea,' said Honey kindly, pushing the false nose humorously up on to his forehead in order to breathe more freely.

'You have a horn on your head. You look like a unicorn.'

'Do I? Does it make you smile? I want to make you smile. You do seem down, today, Morris; go on, smile for me!' He frisked around him, making faces, but Morris did not smile.

In the kitchen, Emily stood at the sink with a carton of caked scouring powder in her hand, a strong girl, a self-sufficient girl who might grow up into a matriarch (or, ignoring the big breasts, which, after all, might be false – a patriarch). With a quick movement, she slit open the carton and scraped out a handful of the hardened cleanser. The pots and pans seemed to fly to her and emerge, sparkling, after she made brief passes over them with her small, strong hands, as in a television commercial for detergents. Already the kitchen looked cleaner and sweet air blew through the window she had contrived to force open. She had wrapped a shirt of Honeybuzzard's round her waist for an apron and, at her feet, her cat clattered around in futile pursuit of flies, spiders, soapsuds. She did not look up when they set down empty cups on the draining board but, when Honey put his tongue lightly on the back of her neck, she wriggled in a very sensual way while saying coldly: 'Get out of it. I'm trying to give the place a good clean-up.'

'Help me to unpack, Morris, my love,' said Honey. His van was filled with crates and cardboard boxes which they hauled into the shop together. From one crate, out fell a large cardboard foot, covered with a toady profusion of cardboard warts. A set of cardboard talons projected from it at the upper end. With a glad cry, Honey picked it up.

'I've always wanted one of these,' he said, clutching it happily to his bosom. A shaft of sunlight struck him, lighting up all his bright colours, turning the false nose in the middle of his forehead into a burning ruby. Morris saw that, quietly, for his own amusement, in some snatched alone moment, Honey had put on a set of false nose-runs, dribbling down from nostrils to mouth in grey plastic tears.

'Plastic snot,' he said in surprise.

'I bought it where I got that phallic rose. Do you like them? On the packet, it said: 'Disgust your friends with plastic nose-drops.''

'Disgust your friends.' I love my love with an H because he is called Honey and his habits are horrible.

False noses (with or without attached moustaches), vampire teeth, false boils, ulcers and pimples, false beards, plastic reproductions of dog excrement (trademarked 'Naughty Puppy' – which he would leave unobtrusively in restaurants and public houses, picturing to himself the discomfort of the next comers), exploding cigarettes (which was why little brown Bruno hated him, for one of Honey's exploding cigarettes had charred his fine, curling moustaches, which were modelled upon those of Salvador Dali – and Honey had sold it to him for marijuana, too). There was no end to the joke-bag, nor to Honey's relish of them. He arranged the world in terms of brutal slapstick, whoopee cushions, rubber fried eggs and blackface soap. 'I should like an exploding contraceptive,' he said once; even sex was a joke, a savage one. Morris wondered if Honey had been laughing when, knife in pretty hand, he had approached – but, no, he did not want to think of that.

He wanted to be amused by the plastic snot. In the old days, before Ghislaine, he had laughed and laughed and laughed at the contents of the joke-bag; nothing else had made him laugh so much. Now, it was more difficult. Still, he managed a small and unconvinced smile. They moved all the boxes into the shop, Honey shuffling in his artificial foot; and then he got bored and left Morris to do the unpacking all by himself.

'I shall make a secret,' he said, installing himself at a table in the back and trailing busily around to assemble a kindergarten paraphernalia of scissors, glue, paper and water-colour paints. Barricaded behind all this, he set industriously to work.

Morris dived through layers of protective newspaper. Hats, boots and artificial flowers; a coronet of paste jewels. As he took out the coronet, a large emerald thudded to the floor. Emily's cat, down from the kitchen to explore, immediately leapt on it and killed it. The corpse of the emerald rolled towards Honey's foot and he, while absorbed in an intricate piece of scissorwork, idly raised his foot and brought it crashing down. The glass jewel splintered. Morris shrugged. He put the spoiled coronet carefully on a knob of the barley-stick Abbotsford chair. He unpacked a velvet robe trimmed with mock ermine; tufts of fur floated to the ground as he unfolded it. After the robe came a pair of white doeskin knee-breeches, suggestively stained.

'H'm,' he said.

'There was this theatrical costumier's,' explained Honey. 'She worked there.'

'Emily?'

'She was trimming a wig in the window. It was a black wig. I knocked on the glass with my knuckles until she looked round.'

'Shall we put all these things up for sale?' asked Morris, delicately

'Not for a while, I think.' That meant they were stolen, then.

'I see.' He scrunched them all back into the box but as he stuffed the crevices with paper Honey cried: 'No, no!' and leapt from his work to scrabble feverishly among the old clothes. He dragged out a curious waistcoat, striped in dull black and purple, with a very shiny black satin back. Morris could see his own face dimly appearing in the back on the waistcoat, as Honey held it up, admiring it.

'Emily says someone wore it in a film of *The Fall of the House of Usher,*' he said. He put on this new treasure, preening the sleeves of his shirt with a great deal of coquetry. He slipped his round fob watch (a silver turnip with an open, honest face) out of the top pocket of the discarded leather jacket and arranged it freshly in the convenient waistcoat pocket under the left nipple, stringing its long, silver chain across his chest.

'How do I look? Splendid, do I look?' In his glee, he shone out with a wide, vaudeville smile, a smile with 'I say, I say, I say, something very funny happened to me on my way to the theatre tonight' in it. He pranced and capered. Morris watched him with – he acknowledged – pleasure. Fancy-dress Honey gave him great pleasure. Nothing had changed.

'You look splendid, yes. But not at all like Roderick Usher, if that was what you wanted.'

'But I wanted to look *doomed*!'

Honey bit his red underlip and brought forward a great, sulky handful of hair over his face. From the neck up, he suddenly became Janey Morris as Guinevere, mouth like a sad pomegranate, cheeks hollowed, shadowed with infinite weariness, infinite experience.

'Is that better?'

'Better.'

Satisfied, he went back to his table. The scissors clicked.

'I like,' he said obscurely, 'I like – you know – to slip in and out of me. I would like to be somebody different each morning. Me and not-me. I would like to have a cupboard bulging with all different bodies and faces and choose a fresh one every morning. And spike a rose in the buttonhole, yes. There was a man, last night; we were in a club and there was this man, singing blues, and he had a red rose stuck in his shirt. It was red as a cap of liberty. . . . I would like to wear him, tomorrow morning. . . .'

Morris said nothing. He continued to unpack. The next box was full of cricket equipment, bats, stumps and legguards smelling of the sweat and warm grass of many summers. He looked at them thoughtfully for a long time and at last put a bundle of stumps in the shop-window, between a plastic washing-up bowl containing old Sunday-school prize medals and a white jugful of paper flowers. 'Who knows; we might sell them,' he thought. 'After all, it is the cricketing season.'

A brush swished in an eggcupful of water. Honey was

painting, now. The white sleeves fluttered. Snow should have fallen from them, they were so white. Morris, curious, prowled nearer the table. Honey gathered all to his bosom, screeching: 'It is a secret! I'll show you, all in good time.'

Morris peered into another box. Horror comics and monster magazines. 'Peril of the fiend women,' announced red letters on one cover. He left the box alone.

The day was clouding over outside. The sun hid behind the clouds and a few heavy drops of rain spattered down. Perhaps there was to be a storm. Morris hoped there would be a great storm with thunder, lightning and torrents of rain, a second deluge; and he would float out, alone, a second Noah, on the ocean-going Abbotsford chair, resolutely pushing underwater the swimming faces imploring him to take them aboard. 'Drown, you bastards, drown.' Oscar. Edna. He paddled on, face turned away, and they sank, trails of bubbles issuing from their mouths. And Honey? Honey's hair waved gently in the water and he was laughing and zip! He changed into a water-snake and coiled round the leg of the chair.

'I shall never be free of him.'

Time passed. It trickled through Morris's fingers in little, ticking, sandy grains. Outside, the rain came down; he could almost hear the poor, dry street sighing with relief. A woman ran along the pavement, soaked cotton dress clinging to her body, holding a newspaper over her head to protect her hair. Nothing else moved but the rain and Honey's hands. Time passed but nothing changed. There was to be no deluge.

And she walked into his empty mind again and sat down. Ignore her, don't think of her – Ghislaine. Think of pretty things, instead; think of white cats and black waistcoats and cheerful Hallowe'en feet. Emily's cat, on cue, padded into the shop from the yard where it had adventured. It carried something in its mouth. It stood in front of the door which led upstairs, mewing as best it could with its mouth full. It had a dead mouse in its mouth.

'Oh, God,' said Morris, oddly near tears.

'Let it out. It probably wants to take the mouse to Emily. It is an intelligent and devoted cat.'

He let the mouse upstairs, sick at heart. At least it was quite dead. Time passed until Honey halted it by crying: 'I've finished! Turn on the light, it is too murky in here to see it.'

Morris turned on the light. Honey held up the object he had been making and pulled a string attached to it. Cardboard legs and green cardboard arms shot out, collapsed, shot out. He had been making a Jumping Jack. The Jumping Jack jumped. The Jumping Jack had a large black head and a small black beard. Morris swallowed; his mouth was full of bitter saliva. The Jumping Jack was Morris. Honey pulled the string once more and Morris's cardboard self convulsed in its St Vitus' dance.

'Isn't it pretty? Isn't it funny?' said exuberant Honey. 'I saw them in London, in a shop full of toys, lovely toys, old toys. I thought I might be a toy maker and make Jumping Jacks and Jacks-in-Boxes and paper dolls and tigers with big teeth that bite when you press down a lever and singing birds!'

Did he not realize what he had done? Did he not realize how badly Morris wanted to hit him and punch him and hurt him? Did he think so little of their friendship – or was it a friendship, what was it. . . .

At that moment, Emily called down that she had prepared a meal and Honey dropped the Jumping Jack as if bored with it already.

'Oh, the lovely girl, she's got us a dinner. Come and have dinner, darling.' He pulled Morris by the hand, eager as a child. There was a cameo head on his poison ring, beautiful and ambiguous as his own head. His touch was warm and dry. The feel of his flesh, the familiar knobbly feel of the ring, the sudden affection in his voice. And so Morris forgave him silently and went upstairs with him. But he thought he would burn the Jumping Jack, when he got the chance.

The light burned on in the empty shop although the rain soon passed and the sun shone again.

6

'I wouldn't mind going to the public house,' said Morris, late that evening, when it was far too late for him to go home. 'I wouldn't feel frightened there if I wasn't by myself.'

'Then we'll all go together,' said Honeybuzzard. 'Perhaps there will be a party on, somewhere, afterwards. I should like to go to a party. I could dance.' He told Emily: 'You must come to the public house, on your first night here. Everybody goes to the pub, you will meet everybody. It's very jolly.'

But the bar, though full, was almost silent, and the first strange thing they saw was the new crop of pimples following the lines of unshaven stubble on the cheeks of Henry Glass as he crouched in a corner beneath a stringless bastard of the mandolin family beached on the wall; and the second strange thing was the flood of tears running down uncared-for cheeks.

'How strange,' whispered Honey. 'He was getting to be so clean.'

Morris questioned a girl they knew, a little blue–eyed girl with long fair plaits now dangling disregarded in her half-pint of bitter. She told them, in a hushed voice: 'It's his wife. She's killed herself.'

More deadpan than Buster Keaton, Honeybuzzard put his hand slyly to his mouth; then smiled, revealing a full set of great vampire stunt-fangs. It was a cruel and audacious gesture. It was his comment.

'You *swine!*' said the blue-eyed girl, Jenny, passionately, and brought her hand cracking across his face. The mark glowed. Honey did not stop smiling. She loved him once. She rolled in his brass bed and told her time by his turnip watch and combed her reflected hair in his dark glasses until he got tired of her and threw her out, when she was still loving him. But she did not love him now.

Morris had not known the dead woman more than to greet her with a wordless smiling when he encountered her, huge and gentle, shapeless as a snow-woman in her pregnancy, buying blood sausage by sign language in the delicatessen or carefully negotiating her laden belly and laden shopping basket along the street. Yet he was unutterably moved.

He pursued Jenny, who had whisked away from them.

'What about the baby?'

'They opened her up and cut it out but it died. He's feeling it, dreadfully.'

'Yes,' said Morris. Henry Glass sat staring at an empty glass before him as if he were practising divination in the patterns made by the tidemarks of froth and could read there nothing but misery. He was a focus of all the world's misery.

'But why did his wife do it?'

'She didn't understand' – she glanced at Honeybuzzard and lowered her voice – 'about you-know-who. And she thought it was Henry Glass who carved up you-know-who and she couldn't bear it, not with being pregnant, and all. No one could read the note she left because it was in Finnish and very badly spelt, too. They had to get the Finnish consul in the end. It was awful.'

'Oh, my God.'

Jenny went to sit beside Henry Glass and hold his cold hand. She did not look at them again.

'Please, don't let's stay,' said Emily urgently. 'We're intruding.'

'It is somebody else's trouble, not yours,' said Honey. 'And they haven't bought up the bar.'

'Still, let's go –'

Henry Glass half rose, then, as if he wanted to speak to them; but slumped back in his chair without opening his mouth. All the people who stood around him turned towards them. They seemed to face a firing squad. Morris's nerve broke and he made for the door. The others came after him, Emily pulling Honey. They survived the line of cold, accusing eyes and got out into the night.

'Ghislaine,' said Morris from the depths of preoccupation. 'Ghislaine. If only I had taken her home with me, none of this need have happened.'

The bar had been a law court; they had stood in the dock. They had been accused. Not Ghislaine but he and Honeybuzzard, or one or both, were held responsible for this irrelevent and meaningless tragedy. Morris, too, accused himself.

If only he had taken the girl home, as he had afterwards thought he ought to do, and snugged her up safe so that she would never have gone, despairing, to Henry Glass. In the dimension where things were done that ought to be done, vast, silent Mrs Glass was at that very minute stirring the supper soup and drawing the snowy curtains of the basement windows to shut the night away from Henry Glass and he had a home and a family and integration and security. But he would never have these things again, in the world where Morris was Morris and could only behave like Morris.

'Who is that? That difficult name?' asked Emily in a muted voice.

'He is talking about a friend of his,' Honeybuzzard told her smoothly. 'Some girl he knows.'

He scooped Emily up and kissed her. At the touch of his mouth, Emily's chiselled face became irradiated with a smile of almost supernatural sweetness. For the first time that day, she smiled properly. She had not smiled properly once before, not from the time Morris saw her first in the café this morning until this time in the blue dusk when Honey told her a lie and kissed her.

They left her in the doorway of the shop, gazing after them as they drove off. The broad, white stripes of her sweater glowed in their vision long after her face was obscured by their distance from her. She would go upstairs without turning on the light and, slipping off her shoes, would lie down on the baroque brass bed she had that afternoon made up with fresh sheets, and take her cat into her arms, pressing it close to her and rubbing her face into its rich, soft fur, over and over again, for comfort (perhaps) – until, finally, it struggled free. The square face impassive, again impassive.

'Poor Henry Glass,' said Morris softly, after she faded away from them. Honey growled.

'Let's have no false sentimentality about the Glasses, shall we?'

'False?'

'You could hardly have picked out the unfortunate Mrs Glass in an identity parade among twelve other women of her size and type and state of pregnancy, especially if they were all carrying shopping baskets, for I never saw her without one. You didn't know her; how can you grieve for her?'

'But don't you feel sorry for poor Henry Glass? And for the baby who will never be born?'

'Don't bother me.'

They drove on in bitter silence. Morris could not keep from picturing Henry Glass's return to the empty basement, stumbling over the scrubbed wooden cradle he had hand-crafted for his child (for that was the sort of thing he did), discovering caches of small garments hidden away in drawers with female undergarments, finding on the bathroom shelf the indescribably pathetic half-used lipstick, the still damp face-flannel.

'It is all getting very sad,' he said at last. 'It is a bad spring, this year. I'm so sorry for them all.'

'They are all shadows. How can you be sorry for shadows?' Honey's voice was harsh. Morris could only see the shadowed profile of the soft-fruit face and, seen in this way, it seemed not soft but a cutting edge, adamantine.

They drew up in a black, deserted street where the lamps made lonely puddles of light on cracked paving stones and walked some distance to a crazy square that stank of rubbish thrown into abandoned areas. Cats, lean and predatory, lurked in overturned dustbins and the blind windows on each side were all boarded. White notices flapped on peeling doors announcing that the city council was about to pull all the houses down. They got out of the van, neither speaking to each other nor looking at each other.

'I wish I could simply walk away from him. He has no heart, he has a computer in his breast. I wish I could just walk away.'

And go home? And go away? And go and try and comfort poor Henry Glass? And go, with grapes or flowers, to poor Ghislaine? And go, with warnings, to poor Emily who smiled with such radiance at Honeybuzzard and did not know how he would treat her, in the end? And go, with his own ragged love tidied into whatever shape he could, to poor Edna? He wanted to take his pity into the world like a missionary.

But the complex of uses to which he could put his pitying heart dizzied him. There were too many; there was too much to pity in the world. He was already weary with all the pitying he had to do. He walked on, down the dead pavements, his head bowed.

There was a veiled moon rising above the houses and the warm night air was thick and brown and heavy as cocoa. Their feet made muffled noises, as if the air was so thick it deadened the noise of their footfalls.

'This will do,' said Honeybuzzard, halting before a narrow passage.

They crept through the passage and into a rank garden patch, still soaked with the day's rain. Their heels squeaked on juicy weeds. With the competence of long experience, they searched smartly over the back of the chosen house for a vulnerable point.

At the first house they approached on this particular night, a dark shaft led possibly to a coal hole; with a shrug, Honeybuzzard, feet first, went down. After a moment, filled with gasps and scraping noises, his face, oddly patched with shadows from Morris's hurriedly struck match, appeared, disembodied, in the vent, as at a seance.

'I'm leaning forward at quite an angle,' he said. 'There is a steep slide, very sticky, but you land on something soft. I think it is coal dust. I hope it is coal dust.'

He rustled and vanished and Morris followed. Down in these bowels, it was warm and moist and smelt of the sharp, clean smell of coal. A wicker basket slowly uncurled itself in a corner and there was an interesting pile of newspapers, tied neatly with string, which they unfastened and riffled through. The magic was beginning to work for Morris. Here in the dark, insulated from the outside life, he read of a brutal murder committed when he was fifteen years old and looked at the time-browned face of the murderer in the photograph and felt secure. He absorbed himself.

Honeybuzzard, meanwhile, penetrated through to the kitchen. He rummaged in a forsaken heap. Tea packets with old ladies in round steel glasses ecstatically sipping from steaming cups pictured on them, old Woodbine packets in William Morrisy greens and purples in curly and ornate squiggles, the striding yellow legs of Sunny Jim and his erect hairdo on a packet that had once contained breakfast food, Force. In a cupboard, beside a time-hardened packet of Epps's cocoa, he found a mice-nibbled straw boater banded with faded school colours of blue and gold. This he put on. His face grew more gentle.

'Tonight, I shall be a song-and-dance man,' he said aloud and split into a water-melon-slice grin.

He found his dark glasses began to impede his progress, snapped them shut and slipped them into his pocket. With his face whitened by the floury light of the candle he carried, he looked bred in the dark, pallid, subterranean. He began to make a pile of the things they might conceivably take away with them. A fat-bellied, black-enamelled saucepan of comfortably Victorian design, obviously intended for the day-long simmering of Mrs Beeton soups, the interior of which badly needed re-tinning. A chipped earthenware pitcher with a primitive slip-wear motif on its pouting breast. A cake-tin produced as a souvenir of the coronation of Edward VII and his queen, whose faces, wreathed in roses, thistles and leeks stared with the modest imperiousness of constitutional monarchs through a web of *lèse-majesté* dust. The stone floor of the long, chilly kitchen struck up coldly through the unmended soles of Honey's boots. He looked around for Morris and t'k, t'k'd with annoyance to find he was not there.

'Time is short!' he called down to the cellar, where Morris sat deep among old newspapers. He stood in the doorway, tipped his boater forward and danced a cakewalk for Morris.

> 'See them shuffle along – yes!
> Scuffle along – yes!
> See dem coons swing and sway,
> Swing and sway the Ol' Miss' way –'

'That is a good hat.'

'Isn't it just? It is a happy hat, my hat for being happy in.'

'Is there one for me?'

'There may be. The people who lived here seem to have kept *everything*.'

They did not find another hat whole enough to be worn, for mice had ravaged almost out of recognition a cupboard full of trilbies, golfing Tyroleans and onion-seller berets under the stairs, but they found a collarless, Steptoe shirt of grey flannel safe in a paper bag, with mothballs tumbling like hailstones on to the floor as they shook it out. Morris fingered the shirt approvingly.

'Lovely bit of cloth,' he said. 'Whoever put it away so carefully can never have thought . . .' His voice trailed away. He was silenced by the poignancy of the care with which the shirt had been preserved for somebody, who turned out to be nobody.

Making small, beaver-like noises in the back of his throat, Honeybuzzard seized a genuine old oil lamp so overgrown with heavy dust that its shape was hardly apparent as it lay on its side in a dim recess and raced it excitedly to the increasing pile in the kitchen.

'In itself, worth the journey! Polish it up and that's twelve pounds ten, to an American!'

They were looking, primarily, for American-bait. In houses the size and age of this one, they looked for small, whimsical Victorian and Edwardian articles that could be polished or painted and sold as conversation pieces. Although there was always the chance of finding built-in furniture i.e. cupboards, corner cupboards, window-seats with backs, etc. that were the age of the house itself and, cunningly extracted from the house, cleaned and polished, could legitimately be termed Georgian or Regency, such finds were rare. Their mainstay was what Honey called '*Observer* Design-for-Living Gear' – aesthetically pleasing tiles from fireplaces; fireplaces themselves and occasional mid-Victorian pottery whimsies like ornately decorated lavatories or wash basins and even chamberpots. They had once, one red-letter day, found a bidet lovingly hand-painted with a pastoral scene of nymphs and shepherds, which they sold to a crew-cut, incredulously giggling, advertising man on holiday from Detroit. They also took early gas fittings that looked charming fitted up for electric light, or so they told people who turned them over in the shop – 'just a coat of white paint, and there you are.' Americans seemed to live in a mad dream of Victoriana.

Oil-lamps, occasional pieces of fine china or pottery or copper pans, or the pile of old prints crumbling in an attic came but rarely and were precious. These were the high spots of their collecting.

And there was the pleasure of creeping through the abandoned dark, of prying and poking. And if that was the real motive for these excursions, then they kept it even from each other and cherished the pleasure separately.

That night, from a business point of view, they were disappointed. The fine fireplaces to be expected in such an old house were all gone, taken by earlier comers, and the only furniture they found, apart from a derelict sofa down on its knees, so poxy with wood-worm bits of it fell to dust at the touch of a finger, was a broken-backed, rush-seated chair of the plain but satisfying, early Edwardian sort. However, one of its legs was badly fractured and the rush-seating was all out, like the littlest bear's chair after Goldilocks had sat in it. After some debate, they decided to leave it where it was.

The bathrooms, all rank and foul, used by many tramps since the water supply had been cut off, were patently post 1914 in date. The only whimsy was a single pottery lavatory chain handle with the blue instruction, 'pull', written on it in an Italic hand, surrounded by a garland of moulded leaves. They already had a whole drawerful of these in the shop and the demand for them was distressingly low but Honeybuzzard loved them and, holding his breath as he approached the excrement choked lavatory, yanked the thing from its chain and put it in his pocket.

In a high room with bars behind its boarded windows, once a nursery, was a raped doll. Someone had stuck its sawdust torso with a knife and all its clothes were gone. But the smug, rosy, wax face smiled sweetly and primly, still, although the golden curls were all wrenched away. Because the surviving smile was so serene and confident, Morris pulled off the head, to take home. It reminded him of somebody but he could not remember who it was.

They carried their candles in single file into a tall, long room, running (probably) the whole length of the building, and saw the points of their flames given back to them in a mirror above the wound where the fireplace should have been. The massive frame of the mirror was richly swagged with bunches of grapes, knots of flowers and ribbons and the horned and bearded heads of small satyrs, whose cloven kicking feet stuck out from clusters of acorns and oak-leaves.

'It is far, far too big to take away,' said Honeybuzzard regretfully.

The glass was clear as a bell, perfect and unflawed and scrawled all over with obscenities, executed in soap. Honey read them all, as far as he could see; then, passing his candle to Morris to hold, he dug in his pocket. He came up with a lipstick, extended it to its full, red length and fired at Morris with it.

'I am no longer surprised at anything you might have in your pockets,' said Morris, unperturbed.

Honeybuzzard drew a large, dropsical, scarlet heart in a free space and transfixed it with a quavering arrow. He paused for a second, tilting his hat backwards and forwards in thought, and then wrote inside the heart, in childish capitals:

'EMILY LOVES HARRISON LOWELL.'

'Why have you called yourself Harrison Lowell? It is an extra-ordinary name to call yourself.'

'It is my real name.'

'I see.' Morris knew very well that Honey was lying. But what did it matter? It was typical of one of Honey's most extreme lies, not an evasion but a simple negation of the truth. 'Is this your handkerchief, or cigarette, or woman?' 'No.' And when such lies were challenged, he would persist in them with insane determination, as if he truly believed in them.

Suddenly he snatched both candles from Morris and set them down carefully on the floor, on the hearthstone. 'Such a fine room, Morris. Such a beautiful room. It could have been a ball-room, all the white shoulders – snowy soft doves of shoulders, nesting in the mirror. Old fashioned waltzes.'

He hummed the first few bars of the 'Blue Danube' and extended his arms. 'Shall we dance? I wanted to dance tonight and so I shall.'

Morris came into his arms and they circled the room. Because of his greater height, Morris found himself taking the man's part and Honey bending himself to the girl's movements. Who was he being now ? A great lady, a grand-dame collecting hearts like butterflies, stabbing them through with her hairpins and keeping them in a glass case? Morris was gradually drawn into the game, too.

Round and round they swayed. Their movements became more and more florid and abandoned. They were dancing at a Grand Ball in the Court of Ruritania, Morris clinking a breastful of medals and flashing two spurred, patent-leather feet, Honey with a king's ransom of diamonds on his high piled hair and another on his snowy breast, advancing and retreating in a tide of swishing petticoats. He flung away his boater after the first circuit of the floor. It skidded across the room like a quoit.

Their reflections merged together, rippling on the dark surface of the mirror that recorded only the intermittent pale blurs of their faces and the gracious, rocking-chair, three-four rhythm of their bodies, spinning between the waltzing walls. Laughing, breathless, they whirled to the invisible rhetoric of a hundred violins. The patches of candlelight illuminated only their feet for odd moments, and then they were back, dancing in darkness again. They neared the extravagant climax of the dance.

'Da – dee dee da – dee da! dum, dum!'

But when the time came for parting and bowing and curtseying to one another, Honeybuzzard instead convulsively crushed his partner in a fierce embrace, pressing his sweating face deeply into the other's shoulder, straining bruising fingers into neck and back, wet mouth fastened on his throat, clinging as if he would never let go until the round world toppled into the sun and the last bell-tower rang midnight and everything was extinguished.

Honey's prickling hair filled Morris's mouth and nostrils with a strong, yellow perfume, the sliding mouth tore his throat. Morris was shocked into incomprehension; he thought he was living in a dream and it was Ghislaine come leaping on to him, come clasping him. In the grip of a panic terror, he exerted all his strength and again and again tried to fling the golden nightmare away from him, battering its body, hearing it cry out, until the grappling fingers relaxed.

Honey slid down to the floor on his knees. He was trembling and there was no colour in his face. He gasped for breath. Morris's eyes slowly cleared; he recognized the other man for his friend. 'What have I done!'

Honey ran his fingers through his hair and shivered. He got to his feet and went to pick up the straw boater. 'My happy hat,' he said. 'But I'm not happy here any more'.

He turned and fled away, out of the room, down the stairs, and Morris followed. The departure became a terrified retreat and involved them both. The house became evil and malignant, out to trap them, and wreak a horrid will on them. They gathered up their few finds from the kitchen, dropping things and cursing, and groping painfully up the vent down which they had slid so easily. But they were fleeing together, now, and they bundled into the van together. Honey drove to the shop at a reckless speed. His teeth were chattering and a nerve in his cheek twitched, but Morris saw he was now in a state of suppressed but extreme excitement.

'I'm going to stuff my Emily rigid,' he said, thrusting the keyring into Morris's hand. 'Take the van, if you want. Or else you've a long walk home.'

He went darting into the shop and the door banged behind him. Morris started up the van. It had been a long day with a strange ending. A puzzle day.

'I need a good night's sleep.'

He remembered, sadly, that he had not told Edna he would stay out that evening and was filled with a doleful premonition of her anguished silence, her speechless recrimination. He dropped off his clothes in the hallway so as not to disturb her and crept into the bedroom. But when the door closed behind him, she said from the bed:

'If that's you, Morris, you can turn on the light. I'm not asleep.' She sounded as if she might be starting a cold.

He switched on the bedside lamp. She surfaced from the blankets in a waterfall of brown hair and clung to his naked arm. Her eyes were raw around the edges and her nose was swollen, but she had not got a cold. She had been weeping into the pillow. Because of him? Who else could she be crying for?

'Edie, I am sorry. I should have sent a message.'

'Oh, darling, I have missed you. Where have you been?'

'Honey and I went out together. He has come home, he came back today.'

But she was not listening to him. Her eyes brimmed and overflowed. She was not, then, crying because of him, for she did not begin to say: 'But there must have been some way of letting me know. . . .' This was serious.

'Edie, darling, what's the matter?'

She rubbed at her eyes. 'You heard about Henry Glass?'

'Yes, I did. It is a tragedy.'

'Oh, Morris.' But she was not crying for Henry Glass; there was something else. She dug under the pillow for a wet handkerchief and blew her nose.

'Morris, I heard about Ghislaine this morning. I met Leonie, Oscar's wife. She was on the bus this morning, going to the shops. And she told me about Ghislaine.'

'Then you haven't heard about Henry Glass's wife –'

Ignoring him, she went on: 'I went to the hospital to see Ghislaine this evening, straight from work. I thought I ought to.'

Fresh tears streamed unchecked. 'This is the second time tonight that I've seen somebody crying,' thought Morris. He gently pressed her hand but she did not return the pressure.

'She was all bandaged up, all her face. Like a mummy. And they have cut off her pretty hair because the nurse said it was such a nuisance and they didn't when she was in there before, because she said she'd do something to herself if they did. And she was hysterical, but she's not hysterical, now.'

'Tell me what's really the matter.'

'I said I was so sorry and could I do anything and she said – she said: "Fuck off, you silly bitch."' Her voice cracked into tears again at the cruel words. 'And she said, why was I poking my nose into what didn't concern me.'

So the poor thing had had her compassion thrown back into her face, had she? Treacherously, Morris thought 'Serve her right.' Spit your compassion against the wind. That's right. But he could see how badly his Edna had been hurt and, after all, she was *his* Edna, and he had to try to make her happy again. He embraced her and cuddled her and sat beside her with his arm around her narrow body until at last she sobbed herself to sleep and the room grew pale with the promise of dawn and the first bird tried out a phrase in the copper beech tree in the road.

7

Emily's mind was like a large, clean, well-lit room in which there was little furniture but that little of the most solid, bulky and hand-crafted kind. If she was largely ruled by her affections, her affections were not casually engaged. Her mind, at that time, was occupied by a large sofa or divan, which was Honeybuzzard; to make room for this new, sizeable and heavy possession, she had shifted out all her other emotional furniture – love for parents, home, the friends of home – and was content, in exchange, simply to be occupied by this present love, and to walk around it, examine it and, in her quiet way, rejoice in it for as long as she might wish to keep it.

For the solidity of her affection did not imply any permanence. Out of sight, out of mind, was Emily's unconscious motto, and just as she had cheerfully thrown away the enormous wardrobe of her father, her first hero, filled with twenty years' accumulation of stored memories and proofs of love, without a moment's hesitation, in order to clear a space for Honeybuzzard, so she might, one day, throw away Honeybuzzard when she came upon something that seemed to her more pleasing, or, perhaps, more in need of a good home.

For she was a charitable girl. Where she loved, she loved entirely; but not, necessarily, for long.

She had a firm sense of occupancy inside her clothes and her strong, well-made body and the firm features of her quiet face. She was always at home in herself. People who had much to do with her came to rely on her a great deal. When she evicted them from her affection, they stumbled off homeless, refugees. Her father stared into his broken-hearted beer nightly (as Henry Glass was doing) since Emily had been away and her pale, insubstantial mother (surrounded by keening babies, tumbling toddlers and restless teenagers) prayed nightly to the Virgin for her speedy return. (They were an immigrant Irish family.)

But the date of her return was not immediately foreseeable, she was installed so comfortably in the Beardsleyesque atmosphere of Honey's shop and his room over it, where the gleaming knobs on the posts of the brass bed nightly throbbed sympathetically and reflected the writhing limbs of the girl and her lover in a miniature, yellow and distorted world. Honey's room might have set a less level and equable girl off balance.

The room was a crystallization of the personality Honeybuzzard presented to the world. One wall was entirely covered with elaborately detailed sepia and white engravings of corset, bustle and hair restorer advertisements lovingly cut from antique magazines. There was a drawing over the fireplace of a woman, a child and a dog in an obscene parody of the Nativity. There was a bust of Queen Victoria wearing one of Honey's ubiquitous false noses. There was a skull from a recently excavated plague pit, which Honey had obtained from a man in the works department of the City Council with the aid of a present of some Indian hemp. There was a collection of matchboxes that the Gloucester firm called 'England's Glory' issue. On the front of these matchboxes is a vaguely patriotic scene of a ship executed in bold red, white and blue; on the back are printed jokes of the 'Who was that lady I saw you out with last night?' 'She might have been out but I was stone cold sober' type. Honey loved these jokes and would tell them over like beads, for hours, laughing.

There was an ailing calceolaria (continually on the point of dying but never quite making it) on the windowsill; it poked out a little, tender, sickly leaf from a dry stem when it seemed that all hope was gone and gave the impression of dissolution indefinitely deferred. Beside this, there stood a jar containing a pickled foetus. There was also a silver-framed photograph of Ivor Novello inscribed: 'All my love and kisses, darling – Ivor'. He was in profile and shining armour, in the role of Henry V.

Morris privately thought that Honeybuzzard tried far, far too hard with this room; every time he went into it, he wanted to cry: 'This is going beyond a joke, Honey.' But he supposed he must decorate it in this wilfully exotic fashion entirely to please himself, for nobody but Morris and his women were ever allowed to see it and he didn't care what they thought. The room was not intended, unlike the plastic nose-drops, to disgust his friends.

The ceiling was painted with black gloss paint. What there was of the walls that showed between the photographs and cuttings were poison yellow; the big mirror at the foot of the bed was placed so that the occupants could see themselves in it, if they so desired. There was a little burner of incense in one corner, which sometimes he would remember to light; it was joke incense, filling the room with the smell of old cheese.

Emily, however, had no particular interest in her surroundings. She disregarded them entirely, making neither comment nor inquiry. Instead, she cleaned them, with remarkable speed and efficiency, and a clinical detachment – as though she were preparing an operating theatre. She disliked dirt. It offended her. One of the reasons why she liked her cat, Tom, so much was because it was always washing itself.

And so was she. She liked her clothes to be always clean, always fresh; if she found a stain on her skirt or sweater, off it would come at once and be plunged into suds for its impertinence, even if she had to walk about in her slip and brassiere for part of the day until the garment was dry. Her underclothes went into soap and water each night and set up a melodious tinkling as they dripped dry over the sink, where, in the mornings and also before she went to bed, she scrubbed her private parts and armpits with a pink flannel upon which her youngest sister had embroidered a lop-sided rose. She consumed a great deal of Lifebuoy toilet soap in a week. Three times a day, she lathered and rinsed her face with her hands, eyeing herself non-commitally in Honey's round, cracked shaving mirror and often she washed her arms and legs as well. She always had the faintly antiseptic spice of soap about her.

Since there were no facilities for bathing at the flat, once a week she would hire herself a slipper bath at the public baths and return home almost transparent with cleanliness. Her hair underwent a vigorous shampooing twice a week and she would sit painting her nails in the shop with a towel in a wimple round her head until it dried. Her legs and armpits were maintained in a continual state of baldness and she bleached the hair on her forearms so that it would not show. She was scrubbed white as her mother's Tooting front-door step. She was the cleanest woman Honeybuzzard had ever had. Her cleanness bewildered and delighted him.

The first thing she did was to take money to buy towels, teatowels and dishcloths. The second thing was to wash, in strong, yellow soap, all the sheets, linen and clothing she could find in the flat. The third thing was to buy a length of material and, in a day, make a dress, since she had with her only her denim skirt and her sweater.

The new dress was of a fine cotton lawn with naive and innocent flower sprigs on a pale pink ground and she gave it a floppy frill around the neck and hem so that she looked as if she had strayed from the striped tent at the end of a 'twenties pier. Poor Pierrot. When she stood beside the horned gramophone in her new dress, with her dark kisscurls and her parting whitely stitched down her black head and so much of her long, long legs showing, Morris thought how strangely pathetic she looked, with such a quality of bitter-sweet, 'twentyish romanticism – a touch of the Michael Arlen. Especially if her hair was hanging down to hide her granite cheek-bone and jaw.

Morris, however, was a blur on her retina; she made this much use of her myopia, that she saw only the things she had decided she wished to see. She tended him when he was in the shop with never a flicker passing across her Red Indian inexpressiveness. She would fill Morris's cup with tea or coffee when he passed it into her limited field of vision, and she would grill him a chop or fry eggs and bacon for him, flipping over the egg in the way she had been told he preferred it, but she performed these services with the competent impersonality of a cafeteria attendant. At first he found this soothing. Then he found it upset him. She was like a well-trained house-robot. And then Honey would touch her and she seemed to fill up and spill over with light. But this rarely happened when Morris was there.

There was not enough room in her mind for friends and acquaintances as well as those she loved. Nobody else had real substance for her, though sometimes she might be interested in something she saw from her windows or even move in a little closer, to see more clearly a landscape with figures. And she would give her charity. Lemonade and chocolate to the children in the street, a smile to an old man waiting for death placidly in the sunshine, a caress to a mangy cat on a wall (swilling her hands in Dettol afterwards). Widely, she gave her charity; yet, impersonally.

When Morris found her in his little workroom, which he normally kept locked, he was startled and uneasy. If she came crashing carelessly into his privacy in this way, she might even destroy it, in the interests of hygiene and the proper use of living space. She stood in the middle of the room, gazing blindly round at all the blank backs of the canvasses lining the walls. She was so fresh and pink and gay in her frilly dress that she made the room look far dirtier than it was, and it was very dirty to begin with. He coughed to show her he was there and she spoke to him.

'What are all these things?'

'Paintings,' he said humbly. The fronts were all turned to the walls and she had no means of knowing.

'Paintings,' she repeated reflectively.

She went down on her knees and began to turn over the pictures, squinting up close to see them. She traced a reflective finger over raised whorls of paint on a spiky, green and white abstract, as if it were Braille and she could read it.

'This one is quite big, reely,' she said.

'Yes.'

'Who did them?'

'I did them.'

She raised her eyebrows as if she had not expected him to be able to make something she could take hold of in her hands. She turned the green and white painting sideways and traced out his name in the corner.

'Yes, there you are. Morris Gray. You painted all these?'

'Yes.'

'It must have taken ages.'

'Yes. It did.'

She looked very stern; he thought she must be thinking: 'What a waste of time.' But, in fact, he had become a little more real for her because she could feel and handle the things he had made. She was as impressed as it was possible for her to be.

'Do you paint naked girls?'

'No.'

'I met this man in this pub and he said he was a painter and would I pose for him. Without any clothes on. He lived in Hampstead?'

'What did you do?'

'Told 'im to stuff 'isself. He was horrible. He had wet hands. But I should have known you were a painter. With a beard, and that.'

Was she, in her inscrutable way, making fun of him? Or was this the real Emily talking, naïve as *Red Letter* or *True Romances*? He could not tell. She went through all the paintings, one after another, saying nothing further. Then she straightened her back and, squatting, examined the grey soles of both her feet, first one, then the other. She licked her finger, rubbed her foot, looked at the dark smear on her hand.

'And I thought I'd cleaned up!'

'It's a bit dirty, here. Nobody but me comes here, usually.'

'I know, it was locked. I found this key in one of his trouser pockets, see, and I thought, you know, of Bluebeard.'

'Bluebeard? '

'Bluebeard. And the locked room. I don't know him very well, you know. And Sister Anne, Sister Anne, what do you see? Nothing but the wind blowing and the grass growing – you know?' She stopped short.

'Do you read fairy stories, then?'

'I was reading it to my kid sister.' Her teeth caught sharply at her lower lip, as if forcibly to stop herself talking so much.

'You got a little sister, have you?' To his astonishment, he realized he was holding what almost amounted to a conversation with her. He had never before exchanged more than two sentences together with her. He wondered how long they could keep going.

'I've got lots of little sisters. And brothers,' she volunteered. She looked coldly at her foot and extracted the suspicion of a splinter, probably picked up from the carpetless floor.

'Big families are unusual, these days.'

'We're Catholics, see.'

'Oh. I see.'

'I think it's all a lot of old rubbish,' she added unexpectedly. 'Catch me having it off without precautions!'

'That's very wise,' he said. He could not think of anything else to say.

A bluebottle flung itself again and again at the dirty window until it at last fell exhausted on the ledge. Its buzz ran down feebly and its legs waved more and more slowly. She picked up a scrap of paper from the floor and squashed the bluebottle dead, raising the paper to display the bellyful of eggs that spilled out of the crushed body.

'There, now. I've put it out of its misery, poor thing, and spared the world from millions and millions of generations of future bluebottles, causing disease.'

'But –'

'I am a practical girl,' she said, and her eyes flashed. Morris kept his eyes from the ruin of the bluebottle. Then Emily spoke again.

'My kid sister, that I used to read fairy stories to, is called Teresa, after rotten Saint Teresa of Avila. Another virgin.' She might have been angling in her memory and brought up this small, spotted trout of a recollection and showed it to him without pride. She added, strangely: 'I can't have any respect for virgins. I don't know why.'

'Were you happy at home?'

She considered this question for such a long time that he thought she had decided to end the conversation without telling him, for her mouth was firmly closed and her eyes as blank as two-way mirrors, out of which she could see though no one else was able to look in. After he had almost given up hope of an answer, she tossed him a minnow from her fish-pond.

'I suppose so.'

He asked stupidly: 'Are you happy here, then, with Honey? Are you glad you came, Emily?'

And she blazed; suddenly she caught fire and her eyes, which were a deep grey, glowed like the sea with sun on it and she said in a never-before heard, rich, vibrant voice: 'I love him, I love him. When he touched me up on Mitcham Common, a man rode by on a bicycle with Catherine wheels, all whizzing with flame, and Honey had set light to them, and he made the moon explode in my head when he came into me.'

Morris actually stumbled back before this barrage of figurative language. He had never heard anything like it before, nor remotely expected such talk from silent, placid Emily. The naked, visionary eloquence of her face was too much for him and he closed his eyes. But, after this revelation, she rose, smoothed her dress and went away. In a few minutes he heard her moving about in the kitchen, through the thin partition.

There was the gush of running water. No doubt she was washing her feet.

He went home straight away and slept for several hours on his lonely bed, badly wanting to blot out the memory of Emily's power of loving. When he woke up, he found his cheek was creased against the chaste frills and small buttons of Edna's nightdress and he gathered it into his arms and hugged it, because he felt lonely. But he could not recapture the flavour of Edna's beige embraces. He thought of passionate Emily enviously, then thought: 'No, I mustn't covet that. Even if he doesn't deserve her. For I wouldn't deserve her, either. And anyway, I too am loved.' But he was not comforted.

After this, he was uneasy with Emily and tried to avoid looking into her eyes; but she was just the same as she had been before.

The incredible summer continued in unnatural perfection. Each day began in a hesitant mist, shaking it off in wreaths and scarves, emerging in the manner of a striptease dancer as the morning progressed; then the nude sun would blaze till past suppertime. The fresh green trees began to curl up and wither at the edges and the grass in the park grew bald and dandruffed with use and refuse – toffee-papers, cigarette ends, matchsticks – of the day's children and the evening's lovers. The weather affected even Edna; her hair lightened a tone, bleached by the irresistible sun, and a gentle tan warmed her face and shoulders a little. She should have looked her best in the summer; but she did not.

There was always something a little wrong with her dresses; too long, so that she looked old and dowdy, or too short, so that she was embarrassed for herself whenever she sat down. Or either they were of fierce reds and blues too emphatic for her pale colouring, or of pastels so insignificant they rendered her almost invisible. Also, Morris took strong exception to the string of chalk-white beads she always wore around her neck, and her flaking, summer-white shoes, which she made a little ritual out of cleaning every night. All the long, light evenings, she sat at the open window quietly sweating into the heap of black wool on her lap, her freshly blancoed shoes drying on the sill beside her, all alone, nursing her lack of company. Morris stayed away from her a great deal these days, but, on the rare occasions when they met, they never mentioned Ghislaine to one another, out of tactful consideration.

'Ghislaine is out of hospital,' said Honey, suddenly, one morning, as he and Morris stripped a chair together in the yard at the back of the shop. 'She's healing up well and she's gone to St Ives.' He sung under his breath in time to the scraping sandpaper:

> 'Oh, don't you hear that lonesome whistle blow,
> That lonesome train-whistle go and blow. . . .'

Morris heard the lonesome train-whistle. Ghislaine had made a take-over bid for his own dream and had boarded his fantasy train and now they scraped a chair in her Troy or Carthage. For an instant he felt thin, spectral and translucent, a figment of somebody else's imagination. He bit purposefully on a carious molar until the pain convinced him he was alive. I hurt, therefore I am. I ought to go to the dentist, therefore I am.

'How do you know she's gone?' he asked.

'She's written me to go with her. But I don't think I will.' He sang again:

> 'My baby sent a letter, addressed it all in red,
> My baby sent a letter, these are the words she
> said. . . .'

The notes went up into the air and dissolved among birdsong.

'As long as Ghislaine's out of town, though!' breathed Morris. 'That's all I want.' They worked away each at his chairleg, companionably. 'If I don't see her, you know, it's as though nothing had changed and this was last summer, before I'd even met her. And perhaps, this time around, I won't meet her. Our paths won't cross.'

'What you suggest is impossible,' said Honey. 'It would be like playing a gramophone record backwards.'

'Maybe I'm getting metaphysical.'

'Christ,' said Honey, and giggled.

His outrageous cap shouted in the sunshine, his dark glasses brilliantly reflected the sunbeams. In the heat, he had taken off his shirt. The lines of his ribs showed through the flesh like an elegant bird-cage where his trapped heart flapped its wings regularly, one, two, on the beat. You could see his navel peering like a surreptitious eye over the narrow snakeskin belt of his white levis, he wore them so low on the hips. He looked like a Mod allegory of summer. Morris crouched by him, still mortifying his flesh in dark, heavy, miserable, winter-weight corduroy. You would have thought he was doing a penance.

He sneezed. Was it the dust from the sand-papering or was he starting a cold? Morris often caught streaming colds in the summer when his eyes and nose ran in rivers. He felt in his pocket for a handkerchief (Edna washed them and ironed them so beautifully that it seemed a pity to desecrate it by blowing his nose into it); in his pocket he found, of all things, a doll's head. He was puzzled until he remembered the night of the song-and-dance hat and the waltzing ballroom. The smug smile between his fingers was, he realized, Honey's smile; this was the resemblance he hadn't been able to place, that between the two smiles. He did not know what to do with the doll's head and put it back in his pocket, in the end. The dark glasses watched him all the time. Morris was embarrassed when he remembered the night of the happy hat. 'And Honey no longer calls me "darling",' he thought. 'Now, why is that?'

'I think I can manage if Ghislaine is far away,' he said, for the sake of saying something. Their work went on.

But there was still Henry Glass, poor Henry Glass. Emaciated, he flitted, almost shadowless, pale as Camembert, through the streets. He could not bear to go back to his basement after his wife's death and spent the night with friends and acquaintances, in informal rotation. The only nourishment he took each day was a nightly cheese roll and half a pint of bitter at the public house. He would allow an eager volunteer to buy his beer for him but always insisted on paying for his cheese roll himself, from a small stock of money that steadily decreased. He was clinging to his independence, the only thing he had left. He clung to the symbolic act of buying his own food with his own money.

Morris could not so much as catch a glimpse of him on the other side of the street without sadness, although he had never liked him very much, in the past. Henry Glass seemed to flicker as he walked, like a silent film, as if his continuity was awry, and he had a look of blank, terrible, absent-mindedness on his face.

'Morris,' said Edna when Morris, for a wonder, was home, once. 'Morris, I asked poor Henry Glass to sleep here, tonight, on the chaise-longue.' She had learned of the tragedy but not from Morris. She had resented him for a little while because he had not told her straight away, until she decided he had only kept quiet in order to spare her feelings.

'I wanted him to sleep on the chaise-longue because he has nowhere to go, not really, but he wouldn't. He said, no, no, he couldn't possibly sleep here, not with us; and his poor hands were trembling ever so much. Do you know why he wouldn't come here. It seems so strange.'

'I don't know, no.'

But it was all of a piece. One morning, little brown Bruno of the shoulder-length curls and fringed jeans ostentatiously walked from the café when Morris set down his harmless meringue at the table where he sat, leaving Morris staring blankly after him with the dead cinders of a damped-out greeting still in his mouth.

The charming Jenny (whom Morris had once partially undressed among a pile of other people's coats on a bed at a party until he thought of Edna, standing palely in the other room waiting for him to return with mythical cigarettes and all at once could go no farther) – the charming Jenny gave him only a worried, fleeting smile when he met her in the public house one lunchtime and asked after her pet mice, of which she had three. (He had explained to her about his wife and she had been solicitous and sorry for him and he had always thought of her as a friend.) They had always talked about her mice, together, before.

Everywhere he went, backs turned and smiles were wiped from faces. If he was with Honeybuzzard, then he received not even the curtest of greetings; no one would speak to them at all, not even if Morris or Honeybuzzard spoke first. People moved away from them. They were, Morris realized, being ostracized. Boycotted. Sent to Coventry. He was irritated rather than upset; it seemed so childish. And Henry Glass went so far as to refuse the offer of a bed. . . .

They would take Emily to the public house together, and sit in a tight, defensive group, and Emily would brutally render the customers into her own distant, chilly perspective.

'Who is that funny little man?' she asked when Bruno, intentionally, jerked Honeybuzzard's arm so that lager slopped all over his shirt (bright pink, that evening, with a button-down collar) and never stopped to say 'Sorry'.

'He is Bruno,' said Honey, slipping an imitation spider into Bruno's unattended half of cider on the next table in retaliation. 'He is partly, I think, Lithuanian. That is his speciality. He is an anarchist.'

'He is far too small,' she judged, 'to be a real anarchist.'

Before Morris's fascinated eyes, Bruno dwindled to the size and futility of a full stop in Lilliput.

'He is a very serious boy,' said Honeybuzzard. 'Morris, do you remember the exploding cigarette?'

'You can't take a man seriously when he's got a moustache like that,' said Emily austerely. She was a hard woman.

During this time, they bought three fringed and beaded Edwardian evening dresses at the auction sale.

'You're out of your perishing minds,' said the overalled porter, tapping his forehead significantly.

'Yes, maybe. But we give you a laugh, don't we?' Honeybuzzard did a little dance for him in a dusty spotlight through an opaque window, holding a mound of amber lace against his breast. His hair swirled at flood-tide.

'You ought to be on the halls,' said the porter, slapping Honey's wriggling bottom.

Honey was disgusted to find that the dresses would not fit Emily, who had a strong, thick-waisted, post-world-war-two figure. So they set the finest one, flamingo satin trimmed with jet, on a dressmaker's dummy whose sadly concave bosom bled sawdust at the touch of a finger, and put it in the shop-window, where no one stopped to look at it.

Morris and Honey began to be extremely busy. Demolition, long deferred, was starting on some of the old houses and time was running short. They went out almost nightly, and, when

Morris returned to the shop with Honey, he would help to unload the night's taking's by the light of the moon, if there was one. Then he would be so tired that he could not think of going home but would curl up with a blanket in his workroom, among the glimmering backsides of his paintings.

Among other things, they acquired in this way:

(a) a quantity of blue and white tiles, possibly Delft;

(b) the dressmaker's dummy that now wore the satin dress;

(c) twenty years of *The Beano* and *The Dandy* in back numbers, which the two men read for whole brilliant afternoons in the solid warmth of the shop;

(d) a Staffordshire pottery dog that, even though its nose was caved in, retained an air of eager inquisitiveness which Morris found so touching that he kept it for himself, in his workroom and even gave it a name, Tray;

(e) a very ugly, dinghy-shaped corner cupboard which they tore from its surrounding plasterwork and eased from a perilous window into the street during the whole course of one perilous night, while Emily kept watch for spies and sneaks.

In the shop, Emily sold a silver decanter label, 'Whisky', for £5 10s to a female American tourist, who proposed to wear it around her neck on a chain. Honeybuzzard, in the intervals of making toys, with which he was now obsessed, sold the pile of moth-eaten carpets to a West Indian for so much more than it was worth that Morris felt badly about it for days. Morris sold nothing; he fought with the desire to paint like Jacob wrestling with the angel. He wanted the release and distraction of painting, yet feared that, in such weather, with so much on his mind, he would paint worse than ever and break his heart by his badness. So he left his paints undisturbed in the cupboard where he kept them.

He sometimes went into the café by himself, to see the singing Struldbrug. He was getting to be fond of her. When she saw him, she put her arms around his neck and sang out: 'How's my darling this morning?' And though he did not think there was really more in her words than playbox affection, she spoke so simply and naturally, with such an effect of spontaneity, that he liked her for it, although she was so old and, perhaps, mad.

8

One morning early, the dregs of a hard night in their mouths, they locked the shop door behind them and stood, sandy-eyed, yawning, among a raped pile of broken crockery; and then they saw Henry Glass swim out of the buttermilk dawn and halt before the window, peering vacantly in. He was no longer anything but a Lowry stick man, spiky and stiff, all in black, and his mouth opened and closed aimlessly in his drowned face where the pustules were blossoming again, since he was no longer eating a balanced diet. They froze in the impenetrable shadows while he shook faintly at the locked door, until he drifted slowly away.

And there followed after him, some moments later, a crazy, silent, dancing crew, faltering, staggering in the ghost light, haphazardly here and there on the pavement, in the road. Among them, Morris made out the truncated shadow of little brown Bruno, and the elongated one of his friend, Shemmy, in battle-dress tunic and bare feet, his long, long hair caught at the nape with a draggled ribbon, and the spare, hopping mosquito with the pin-point head, Okum, registered as a drug addict and proud of it. There were other men and also some women.

One of the women paused theatrically and threw back her head, pealing with ringing laughter of which they heard but a faint echo, where they hid in the back of the shop. She had a round, white face and round, brown eyes with a tinge of red in them and had infected Honey with gonorrhoea two years previously.

The gang drew into a ragged group outside the laundry and with one accord turned and faced the shop. Some whispering went on, now, and some gesticulating; then one of them – Morris could not see who – pitched a brick at their window. The missile went wildly astray, shattering itself to smithereens against the metal plate above the door, but as if at a signal, they all, shouting (though the two men could hardly hear them, through the thick glass) surged across the road at the very moment when the streetlamps went out. They carried sticks and stones and broken bottles and pieces of wood with nails in them and Morris thought he caught the flicker of the blade of a knife.

Then the ponderous bicycle of a patrolling policeman rolled majestically down the road and they all ran away, just like that, in a clatter of dropped, scared bottles, flapping their black wings and cawing.

'High,' said Honeybuzzard. 'Higher than larks. Can't even throw a brick straight, my God.' His contempt was fierce and withering; it curled his mouth like a lemon.

'All the same . . .' Morris's voice sounded squeaky and unnatural. 'I . . . it was . . .' And his voice trailed away. He played with the bead fringe of the flamingo satin dress, knotting and unknotting it, until Honeybuzzard snapped: 'Will you stop fidgeting?'

'What would that rout have done to us?'

'Nothing. I would have told them to go home and they would

have gone. They were too high on drink or drugs or whatever that they couldn't have kicked a baby and would have obeyed any firm order.'

Morris, abstractedly imagining the crimson garlands of his guts splashed and gleaming across the yielding floorboards, did not believe him.

'But they wanted to kill us, I think. You and me.'

'Oh, don't be silly. I was quite enjoying it, that sort of thing doesn't happen every day, does it? It's all part of the rich fabric of life, isn't it? I've never been under seige before.' He laughed, quite naturally.

'But why did they come here? They aren't even the "Gloucester" people. Most of them were the ones who go to "The Cornet of Horse". Okum goes there.'

'Henry Glass called out all his friends to come and help him right his wrongs on us, I suppose. And they all turned out; it's rather touching.'

'They never used to be his friends. And they weren't with him, they were tagging along behind.'

'They're friends of Bruno's, and Henry Glass knows Bruno. And Henry Glass doesn't seem in a state to make fine social distinctions these days, does he? Were you really afraid? How odd.'

'I was very frightened yet it seemed unreal, somehow, like a dream,' said Morris, slowly, considering. 'But, yes, I was frightened. Oh, God – poor Henry Glass, though!'

'I love my love with an H because he is called Henry and he is heartbroken.'

'I shan't sleep tonight.'

'Go and play patience, then,' said Honey sharply. 'For I'm going to bed.'

'No – don't leave me alone. Please.'

Honey took off his dark glasses (even at night he wore them) and began to polish them. 'Say "please", again, nicely, and I'll think about it.'

'Oh, Honey, please stay with me! Just for a while. They might come back. Stay.'

He put the glasses back on and smiled with feline self-satisfaction. 'Let's play chess, then.'

'Chess? I haven't played chess for years.'

'I shall beat you, then.' He dug in a box and produced a board and a wooden box of men. Morris had never seen the chess-set before but Honey stroked them as if greeting old friends. He set out the pieces tenderly.

'First the castles, one at each corner, like the legs of a cow. Then the knights – I love the knights; such proud horseheads, such flaring nostrils and, besides, they move obliquely. Now the reverend gentlemen, next to the caballeros. And the Queen, the travelling lady; she's my favourite piece, she can go anywhere on the board – zip, zip. And a femme fatale, she is, whose kiss is death. Uneasy lies the head that wears the crown, here is the King. Vulnerable, your King – in the last resort he has to hop off one by one, stage by stage, like Louis XIV escaping from Versailles. Morris shall be black and I white. There are our infantry, our pawns, all ready to go over the top. Let's begin.'

They sat on opposite sides of the table and moved their first pawns. The pieces were old and large, fitting comfortably in the hand. The ancient and hieratic game soothed Morris very much; he remembered he had once loved to play chess, because it always took such a long time. He drew first blood; he took a pawn. Honey rolled a cigarette and meditated his next move.

'I should like,' said Honey dreamily, 'to have a floor set out in chequers and to play chess with men and women. I would stand on a chair and call out my moves from a megaphone and they would click their heels and march forward. The knights on real horses, the royal couple with gold crowns on their heads.'

'What would you do with the pieces that were taken?'

'Put them in cages, the fools. Look, I have brought my knight out of the stable. See how he leaps.'

Honey check-mated Morris in ten minutes; but Morris had begun to get the feel of the game again, and, in the second game, soon took Honey's Queen. Honey howled: 'You can't take my lady!'

'Oh, yes, I can,' said Morris, and he grinned and put her in his pocket. He was beginning to enjoy himself.

Their bloods began to rise. After a quarter of an hour, Honey, who had begun to play from the emotions rather than from the head, was forced to send his King sceetering around the board in an undignified manner, pursued by two of Morris's pawns and one black knight; they had fallen into one of the deadly chess impasses, where one side can only attack and the other only defend. Morris was so absorbed he could not see Honey's growing agitation. During a strategic pause, Honey managed to threaten Morris's own King with a surviving castle but Morris scornfully stormed the castle with a cunningly reserved bishop and swept it off the board. They began to breathe heavily. Honey began to edge his last knight into the offensive, but, before it could become a threat, Morris let out a crow of pure glee.

'Pawn to the back line ! Pawn to Queen, like in *Through the Looking-Glass*! You might as well give up, now.'

With a sob, Honey rose up and overturned table, chessboard and all.

'You're cheating, you're tricking! I won't have it, I won't have it, you can't have another Queen, you can't!'

The pieces went this way and that, all over the floor. It was now broad day and early-rising Emily opened the door on a tableau of Honey lying in the Abbotsford chair with his chin quivering like a baby's, blowing his nose on a tangle of peacock feathers, while Morris searched for chessmen on his knees. Emily stared coldly.

'We – we were playing a game,' said Morris apologetically.

'Silly sort of game to get so worked up about it.'

She went away to put the breakfast on and Morris turned the table right side up and began to put away the chess set.

There was a smell of bacon from upstairs and the brown hint of toast by the time all was put straight. Honey sniffed himself calm and did an unusual thing. He sidled up to Morris and lisped in a baby voice: 'Honey thorry.' He could only say he was sorry by pretending to be a sorry somebody else.

'That's all right,' said Morris. 'We are overwrought, both of us. It was those people, coming like that.'

'I kinda hoped you'd forgotten them. But I behaved badly. I will be good, today. I will do something quiet. I shall make more toys. I am working on a little toy guillotine, Morris; a razor blade in a frame, powered by a rubber band. Emily can play Madame Defarge and sit and knit and I will make a tiny figure of Bruno out of pipe-cleaners and kneel him down and off with his head! And he will vanish.'

But it was not as easy as that. That evening Honey and Emily went to bed early, to make love, and Morris did not want to be alone downstairs in the shop with the memory of the attack. He went home, for the first time for some days. He found he wanted to share the experience of the previous night with Edna (a trouble shared is a trouble halved) but she seemed oddly unsympathetic to him. There was a pervasive unease in his house; something was wrong, a flavour of wrongness as elusive yet unmistakable as that of sour milk in tea.

Edna smiled often, a trembling, watery smile, but scarcely spoke to him and her hands shook a little as she served the food and she turned away her head if she thought he glanced at her. He thought that perhaps his hard-working nights were beginning to bring her down, but he did not wish to raise the subject of them with her.

She had ceased work on the big sweater for some reason she did not tell him. He was too thankful for it to mention the unaccustomed idleness of her hands in case she took it into her head to start on it again, thinking he was complaining. So they had a silent evening.

As always, these close nights, when he slept with her, even the blankets weighed too heavy on her and they slept far apart on distant sides of the bed so as to generate by contact as little clammy and wakeful heat as they could. She was not in the mood for sex, these long, hot nights. She would sigh and put on her martyred smile (St Ursula, the virgin, smiling at the rapists; painted by Burne Jones, rather than Millais for in the heat she grew waxen and moist-looking at once) and weakly clasp her long hands and say that if he wanted her, very badly . . . And he would feel a crude unfeeling brute and master his at best feeble and tepid desire. Because she would have done a thing so abhorrent to herself, merely to give him a crumb or two of pleasure, and it was a lesson in self-control to him.

But that night he sweated and could not sleep, thinking of Honey and Emily rolling in the brass bed.

In the days after the little siege, he became heavily involved with a new fantasy. He thought how nice it would be to be invisible and, to his surprise, sitting uncomfortably in the Abbotsford chair, he became so through the force of his imagination. It was a very vivid fantasy and he indulged in it more and more often. He would sit in the big chair and all his flesh would dissolve, while Emily pottered about the shop with a feather duster like a maid in a French farce, a spotted handkerchief about her head, or stripped the silver from her hands and feet with sharp-smelling acetone, and Honeybuzzard played quietly with his toys upstairs.

Morris would dissolve. Liberated – for somehow he associated invisibility with a lightness and airiness of body, so that he floated above the streets and soared with airy lightness from place to place – he would first of all do the happy, child-like things. He made a little home for himself in the Romany caravan in the museum, sleeping among the cut glass and the mirrors engraved with bulging swags of grapes, or sit at the controls of the fire engine, or curl up in an embryonic position in the rib-cage of the great elk.

And then he would do the perverse things. Succubus-like creep into the wombs of sleeping women, the sleek and unapproachable women who wore wide straw platters on their heads and took morning coffee in the Regency Room restaurant of the departmental store, with pet dogs on their laps and bracelets of semi-precious stones a-clank as they stirred coarse brown sugar into demi-tasse and lit their king-sized, tipped cigarettes with gold lighters. And tangle the luxuriant hair of Oscar's wife, snagging the dark undergrowth of it unbearably as she tried to back-comb it into the Madame Butterfly pagoda she wore on her head . . . and father a cuckoo child on her to grow up in Oscar's nest. And slip cantharides into his own wife's morning tea, so that she gave herself, yelping, to the milkman. And he would do many other things, as he sat in the shop, invisible.

Once he imagined that, as he slipped invisible across a busy road, a lorry filled with high-pitched piglets ran him down and no one could hear his invisible screams or could see the bright flow of his invisible blood or witness his invisible death agony. He came back to his flesh, choking and crying out.

'What's biting you?' asked imperturbable Emily, mending a long, white sock.

'I was just . . . dreaming. . . .' He wondered anxiously if he was becoming psychotic. 'Do I need therapy?'

So finally he forced himself to paint a picture. He took blacks, browns and a bitter blue and intended it to be abstract but it became figurative under his fingers; a decaying female form, dead, in a brown desert, under a cruel blue sky. Though he disliked it intensely, he could not stop it growing under his fingers. 'I *am* becoming psychotic.' But perhaps it was best to work it out on hardboard.

Emily crept in to watch him, after he had spent a whole day locked into his workroom, not even coming out for lunch. For a time, she seemed almost hypnotized by the strokes of the brush and sat on the floor watching his movements. The cat came in with her and picked delicately among the pictures and rubbed its head against Morris's ankle. Getting no response, it rolled over, stuck a hind leg in the air and began to furiously wash its genitals. Morris mounded black on brown.

'You're married, aren't you?' she asked.

'Well, yes.' The woman-shaped lump wanted to be textury, feely, to jut, hunchbacked, swollen, from the surface. He alternately coaxed and battered at the paint.

'Are you nice to her?' He stopped painting and looked at her in surprise. But she was too cool and objective with her question to be offensive so he replied as honestly as he could, haltingly.

'Yes. No. I don't know.'

'This man. He came in yesterday afternoon, while you and Honey were out somewhere, I forget where. He pretended he wanted to buy one of these big, black tea-caddy things but he didn't, really.'

'We do charge a lot for them, I suppose,' said Morris guiltily.

He always felt guilty about taking money for the things they sold.

'He wouldn't have had one for twopence. He just wanted to chat me up. He said that you were very cruel to your wife and that she was a shadow of her former self since you married her and how could I bear to work with a man like you. So I was interested, you know?'

'I see.' Some attacked by night and some by day. He laid down his brush. Then it was Edna who was struggling out of the picture on his easel.

'It was that fat man, the one you and Honey were sitting with the day I came here, in the café. I knew him but he didn't know me. And he said he had a special message for you and I was to tell you carefully. It was, "Edna is the best woman in the world but you neglect her and don't know her. Why, only the other day, when you were God knows where, she persuaded Henry Glass to eat his first hot meal for days. She is a good woman." He made me repeat it twice, to make sure I got the words right. What does it mean?'

'I don't know.' Oscar's manner of speaking filtered through Emily's flat voice; Morris could hear him behind her.

'Then he said he had some photographs to show me, because he didn't think I knew either you or Honey very well, and that I ought to. But that little kid came in because it wanted to use our toilet and I suppose the fat man got fed up with waiting for me, because he went, after that.'

'I see, yes,' Honeybuzzard sold the photographs of himself and Ghislaine for £5 the complete set, very cheap. Oscar bought them, saying as he paid over his notes that Honey had no head for business.

'He was a horrible, creepy man, all sweaty. He had his shirt open and this string vest and all this hair on his chest. Honey hasn't got hair on his chest. I could never, you know, fancy a man with hair on his chest.'

'Why didn't you tell me this before?'

'I wanted to have a brood about it. I mean, I don't know either of you very well, really; he was right.'

Honey was watching the shop. Paper, paints and string (more Jumping Jacks?) were discarded on the table while he tried on a pair of steel-rimmed glasses, gazing at himself in a small mirror with a bulbous cherub on top of it that he had propped on the stuffed carp. He took a swatch of his hair and piled it on top of his head, goggling through his round bottle glasses at himself. He pinched his lips together and sucked in his cheeks. He became a virgin schoolteacher, mistress of maths or classics, withering as if pressed between textbooks in some ivied, select girls' boarding school, from whom the pubescent females had extracted all the lingering sex. He patted a curl he had made with spit on his forehead. Morris took all this in.

'Honey, Oscar has been here. She's been thinking about it; she's only just told me.'

'Who is she? The cat's mother?' Honey spoke in a pedantic, high-pitched, cracked and querulous voice. Obviously, he intended to carry this impersonation through. Morris wondered how far. He could take no pleasure in this particular transformation.

'He was trying to set Emily against you, I think. He wanted to show her those pictures.'

'And so? And so? I spit me of Oscar.' He tore off the glasses and the schoolteacher, thank God. But he was hard, today.

'Why should he care? It was like the other night. They are all in it together.'

'It doesn't bother me. Sticks and stones may break my bones but words can never hurt me and I don't care about sticks and stones.'

'Emily's too nice a girl for all this. And the shop used to seem so safe.'

'Emily's old enough to look after herself. She used to sleep with rhythm and blues singers. And I'm still safe here. Anyway, I'm making Oscar into a Jumping Jack. That should take care of him.'

Sure enough, there was Oscar on the table, all in bits, round head, round body, great limbs. And there – Morris caught his breath – was Ghislaine, not yet cut out but drawn and coloured in segments on paper, all scarred.

'And her, too? You can do that?'

'Why not? She always did jump when I pulled her string, poor little girl. She sent me another letter, addressed all in black, she sent me another letter – baby, I'm coming back.'

'Christ! When?'

'When the leaves turn yellow.' He sang, in an atrocious French accent:

'It's a long, long time, from May to December,
And the leaves turn brown . . . (is it brown, I forget . . .)
The leaves may possibly turn brown when you reach September . . .'

He shook down his hair and it danced, shaking out with tinselly lights. He poked the steel-rimmed spectacles ferociously into the somnolent stomach of the cat, who harmlessly slept on a flattened cushion on the floor.

'That's the monstrous birth gestating in the womb of time,' he said, and laughed.

'Are you telling lies, or what? Is she really coming back? I can't tell, you're in a difficult mood today.'

'Believe what you want to believe. What you want to believe is the truth'.

'What the hell does that mean?'

'They, the shadows, think you held her down while I wielded the knife. Fine, wonderful, perfect. But I think I ran for a doctor and you sopped up the blood with your nice clean hanky when we found her, poor little girl, among the gravestones. Maybe, though, we should have left her there and then that Scandinavian woman would be having her baby, wouldn't she? A life for a life, that's how it goes.'

He began to tease the drowsy cat with the spectacles, holding them out and wiggling them temptingly and withdrawing them as it began to feint at them with a lethargic paw. Morris was confused and bored. He shrugged and slipped out into the street. Honey, absorbed in his game, did not speak.

Morris bought cigarettes at the distressed newsagents, pushing through the doorposts on which fluttered out-of-date copies of *Woman's Own* and weatherbeaten *Tit-Bits* and copies of *Sporting Life*, all tanning slowly and curling open like flowers in the rays of the sun.

Inside it was cool, dark and deserted and he clinked his half-crown against the top of a jar of corroded soft-centred fruit drops for some minutes before she came from the back, shutting the glass-topped door on a faint moaning;

'How is he, today?'

'Not too good, not too good at all. What do you want?'

As she dispensed with her customers one by one, so she dispensed with traditional shopkeeper's courtesy to the few who remained.

'Ten – no, twenty Woodbines.'

'Two tens do? All we got.'

'Fine.'

The translucent salmon-pink overall which she wore wilted in the heat, hanging open over her slumping breasts only partially concealed by a white blouse, buttoned all crooked. Her clothes no longer seemed to have the energy to cover her properly. She was as featureless and indistinct as the figures on the worn pennies she gave him for change; her twiggy fingers seemed hardly able to manage a lumpish threepenny bit and the slippery sixpence slid through her thin thumb and fingers, escaping from her and vanishing among the lost days of last week's *Radio Times*.

'Dear, oh, dear!' And she had to shake it out, slowly, wearily, to retrieve it for him. The pages sighed.

'You look as if you could do with a nice rest in bed yourself,' he said gently. 'With someone to look after you.'

'I shan't get no rest till he goes –' moving her head towards the door and the faint groaning behind it that never ceased. 'It's a hard life.'

'Yes,' said Morris. 'It is.'

'Mother,' groaned the ravaged voice. 'Mother'. They had no children but he always called her 'mother'.

'I must be getting back to him; he needs me. Nothing else, dear?'

'No. Nothing else.'

A dog raised its leg to pee against the rusty sign that announced the tobacconist also sold a certain brand of ice-cream. Over the way, the laundry digested its day's diet of filthy linen. The cigarettes tasted stale and somehow dead.

Morris went to drink a glass of milk. He thought it would do him good and he thought it would also do him good to see the singing Struldbrug. She welcomed him warmly with a chorus of 'Some Day my Prince Will Come', and he was momentarily a snug child in a nursery where red coals glowed behind the disciplined fireguard and the air was sweet with the smell of ironing and bread and milk. But the café, in the dead middle of the late summer afternoon, was filled with old ladies taking a break from hard shopping.

Stuffed in cylindrical straw hats, surrounded by baskets, sticks, paper-bags and small dogs, they sucked cautiously at dainty toast fingers for fear of breaking their porcelain teeth and conversed in little voices, stop and go as clockwork mice. Old ladies, especially if they appeared unloved, always scored a direct hit on Morris's soft heart and he left the cafe hurriedly for his heart had already taken sufficient beating from the tobacconist's wife for one day.

He went to look at the Japanese porcelain in the museum. He had never looked at it before; but now seemed a good time, for he had always associated the Japanese with tranquillity. In tranquillity, they ceremoniously prepared and drank tea, performed endless stylized dramas, arranged tranquil flowers full of Zen and did tranquil water-colour paintings which left three-quarters of the real world out, thus, through tranquillity, annihilating temporal existence. So he went to look at the porcelain. But it did not do him much good.

9

The nights were lengthening and cooling. More and more often, when they entered a house, they found that the horse and cart totters had been there before them and gutted it bare. That night, in one tall house, they searched from cellar to attic and found only a bundle of bloodstained rags and a picture of the Queen in a red jacket on a brown horse, tacked to a lavatory wall. However, there was a skylight on to the leads, through which they ascended, and so gained access to another house which proved to have been left untouched.

It had been deserted in a great hurry. There were heaps of crockery and clothes tumbled everywhere, drawers and shelves emptied of their contents and tipped on the floor, jettisoned to lighten the labour of removal and finally completely abandoned, in a fit of pique.

Curtains still hung, layered with dust, at the windows; a chamber-pot, rank with urine and floating a crust of dead flies, stood in the centre of an attic floor; a burst handbag someone had thrown against a wall spilled photographs. Morris went through them curiously. A young woman in a strange hat like a mangled dove smiled shyly at the camera; two sailors in uniform had their arms about each other's shoulders and must surely be dead, for they both had the look in their eyes that one finds in early photographs of Rupert Brooke, elegiac and somehow fated. And there was an old powder compact half out of the bag and its mirror cracked. Seven years bad luck for somebody. Morris superstitiously closed the compact and slipped it back in the bag. They left the top storey.

The house grew increasingly odd as they descended the stairs. There was a framed text, 'Love thy Neighbour,' illuminated with lilies, drunkenly askew over a doorway and, inside, a snaggle of rosaries in a corner beside a pillow with brown, downy feathers drifting from a rent in its ticking. It was a small roof, too narrow for its height, sweltering in its closed-up heat.

Honey picked over the pretty strings of beads excitedly, lopping red and black glass currants round his wrists and neck and plaiting them through his long hair, while Morris opened a built-in cupboard and found piles of hymn-books, prayer-books, worn and loose-leaved, and a water bottle, empty, with a glass inverted over it and a soft little brown rag, all forlorn, which proved to be a dead mouse, lying beside it.

'Poor mouse.'

'Mmm?'

'A dead mouse. With the prayer-books. It was a church mouse.'

'Fattened, you mean, on consecrated bread and the stubs of holy candles, staggering drunk on dregs of the host? Or a holy mouse, like holy cows? Do I look pretty?'

He gestured gracefully with his heavily decorated wrists and arms and slowly turned his laden head this way and that, like a Javanese temple dancer. In the candle-light, the red beads shone like poison berries.

'You look like an illustration to "Goblin Market".' Morris

dropped the mouse into the water-bottle and stoppered it once more with the glass, from a vague instinct to put it away tidily. He closed the cupboard door on it.

'What can have gone on here, though, Morris?' In spite of the care with which Honeybuzzard rose to his feet, the beads slipped out of place and rained, pattering coolly, straight down to his feet. Suddenly bored with them, he kicked them aside and tugged the rest off his wrists and threw them about the room.

'I can't think. Perhaps some sort of religious hostel?'

'You mean, rows of virgins in little white beds?'

'Perhaps that sort of thing, yes.'

'But we haven't seen any little white beds. And there's not the tiniest whiff of any lingering smell of virgins.'

'What do virgins smell of?'

'Bread and butter. But the very best bread and butter. Not that I've smelt any virgins, not lately. Not since they published *Lady Chatterley's Lover* and opened the floodgates of corruption.'

In the next room, a Christ with a girlish waist and arms as long as his legs stretched taut on a crucifix torn or fallen from the wall. His plaster nose was chipped, there were cobwebs in his beard and Honey's booted foot crunched a hand to dust in the darkness. He stooped with his candle to see what he had trodden on.

'So sorry, old chap.' He raised his candle and looked round a bleak, white-painted cell, with a grille over the window. 'Oh, God, there's plenty here but nothing to take away.'

'It's nice here, though. It's eccentric.'

Honeybuzzard knelt to examine a bundle of clothing. 'Just aprons and overalls the cleaning women must have left behind. Here's one with a used bit of Elastoplast in the pocket, all rolled up.'

'That's poignant, isn't it; a used bit of Elastoplast.'

'It's too new to be poignant. It's disgusting.'

Morris picked up, examined and discarded a plastic lily. 'This *is* an eccentric house.' He picked up and discarded a plastic holy water stoup.

'Perhaps we could have a party here,' suggested Honeybuzzard.

'We don't know enough people to ask to a party,' said Morris. 'Not any more. Nobody knows us. It would be a lonely party.'

'Ghislaine would come. We would take it in turns to lay her on that chap there.' He indicated the inoffensive Christ. 'She would like that. And we could take pictures and sell them to the colour supplements.'

'Don't joke about her. Please.'

'It would be interesting, though, to see just how far she'd go before reaction set in. I always used to feel that she was trying to be so wicked, yet all the time . . . you know her father's a clergyman?'

'I didn't, no.'

'But it seems obvious, when you do know, doesn't it? She could only be a clergyman's daughter.'

'Please don't talk about her, Honey.'

He took off his dark glasses and polished them. His slithery eyes went up and down Morris. Morris expected to find himself covered with a snail-track of slime, so closely, closely, in such a reptilian way, did the eyes go up and down.

'Did you know she wrote me that it was like a spiritual defloration when I knifed her? That is what she said, in purple ink. Her prose is getting a bit florid. But a spiritual defloration! It made me wish I had done it.'

'Please. It's nauseating.'

'No,' said Honey, considering. 'No. In a way, it's funny. But chaining her to that symbol of her father over there and raping her – now, that would really be something.'

'Put on your glasses, for God's sake, and shut up. You're crazy.'

They descended another staircase and crept into a room which, they gradually saw, contained a few skeletons of folding chairs, some with legs and canvas backs still sticking up pathetically from the floor, like broken butterflies, and a shelf-ful of candles, some of which they providently took with them, and a bent little doorway which led to a dank little scullery with jars and pots and a sink in it, perhaps a room where, once, flowers had been arranged.

'And then the top floor, so full of the signs and life – pisspots, and that. I don't see how it fits in. What did go on here.' Morris was perplexed.

'Perhaps it was sub-let. Or they kept the domestic staff there. The religious life has always got to be heavily based on the irreligious one, or it can't survive, can it?'

They went down to the basement, each shielding his little flame, moving in two tiny spheres of light. The basement kitchen was a long, narrow room with a black range filling one end and a stone basin into which dripped water from a green brass tap. It smelt most terrible – of damp, of rot, of excrement, of mice, of rats, of garbage, of age, of hopelessness, of uncleanness, of decaying stone, of crumbling wood, of soot, of human physical corruption and of the physical corruption of old houses, all mingled together in one gigantic, overwhelming stench.

'Smell of tramps,' said Honeybuzzard.

They stood before the tall dresser, holding their candles high to see if any plates or pots remained forgotten on the farthest shelves but there were only shadows. Slowly, the two patches of light travelled down. And finally, on the surface of the dresser itself, Morris's candle illuminated in dramatic chiaroscuro a heel of loaf, a rind of cheese and a tin of condensed milk, the open lid pushed down to protect the contents.

Morris picked up the tin as if to verify its existence by touch, for he half refused to believe in it. The tin adhered stickily to his fingers. The milk was fresh.

'Signs of tramps,' repeated Honeybuzzard.

Then they found a bed, an insubstantial camp bed that hid in shadows as if it was ashamed. It had a grey army blanket tucked in and around the edges for a coverlet, stretched smooth and neat, and sheets – damp sheets, they felt them and wiped their fingers – turned invitingly down over a hard, hard pillow. There was folded clothing in the drawers of the dresser and a little old cracked mirror on the mantelpiece with before it a pale blue plastic comb with a good deal of hair caught in its teeth. The hair was pepper-and-salt colour. All this they found out by bits and pieces, in furtive sorties.

'This is far too tidy and premeditated for a tramp, Honey. Someone lives here all the time.'

In this hole.

Beneath the bed was a pair of shoes, symmetrically arranged side by side; once black, now grey and slightly mildewed, the shoes, over the years, had cracked and swollen to fit the corns, bunions and wens of the feet of an elderly woman and were misshapen and surreal. Tucked inside each one, curled up cosily, sleeping, was a mouse-coloured woollen stocking.

'Someone who lives here is female.'

The atmosphere of the basement room was so moist that there seemed to be droplets of water suspended in it, as in the fen country, and breathing was a battle. Submerging, they gasped for breath and their mouths filled with the odour of all the rots in the world, mineral, vegetable, fungoid, human.

'If we had a canary in a cage, it would drop down dead,' said Honeybuzzard in a low voice. His bright colours were fading; the air was too bad for him to bloom and he was withering.

The windows were not, as they had first thought, boarded up

but hidden by sturdy shutters from which the paint was peeling, leaving continents, islands and archipelagos of raw wood that had the quality of untreated wounds. A scroll of whitewashed paper hung from the ceiling, scattering light, white dandruff over the floor and there was further evidence of habitation in a corner, a round, horny, primitive gasring by the range, and above it a gas bracket, with a lint-white, lint-clean, brand-new mantle upon it.

'We are burglars,' suggested Morris. They stared at each other. The candle flames blanched their faces and made the shadows huge, moving, threatening. 'We must go away. We've never been burglars before. Everywhere else, there was nobody.'

As Morris moved towards the bare boards of the door that had a great iron latch, the 'lift-up-the-latch-and-walk-in' latch of nursery tales, they heard slithering footsteps on the area steps outside and a voice raised uncertainly in indecipherable song. He froze in his tracks with fear and apprehension, eyes and mouth open like a Greek mask of horror. There were wheezings and bangings at the door and the jutting latch jiggled; the sound of a push, breath, effortfully expressed, wood grating on stone.

Suddenly the door, out of control, swung open and banged against the frame. A gust of sweet night air blew into the room and was immediately extinguished by the black breath indoors. Their candles blew out. A finger of light from a street lamp out-side widened into a cone and was then blotted out by a large, dark, lumbering shape, sighing and moaning and rancid.

It brushed past them but by some miracle did not touch them. Morris wanted to run for the door and escape but as he stirred, he felt a cold hand on his wrist. He nearly cried out; but he felt the familiar ridge of Honey's poison ring against his palm. Honey was stopping him. Honey wanted to stay.

The figure upset a boxful of matches with many small, rattling sounds and breathed 'ee, dear, ee, dear', as she creaked down on her knees to pick them up. Morris pulled sharply at the firm, insistent hand and it let go of him. He reeled for a moment and clattered against the pathetic camp bed just as Honey flared out the flame of his enormous cigarette lighter.

Blearily, dreamily, uncomprehendingly, the woman on the floor turned her drunken, midnight face round towards the noise and the light. Morris, with a terrible pain, saw that she was the old woman from the café, who sang to him.

In the flickering blue light, Honey's long, pale hair and high-held, androgynous face was hard and fine and inhuman; Medusa, marble, terrible. A little wind through the door blew about his flame so that the light seemed to stream from the ends of his whipping hair. She gaped up, baffled, wondering; like the Virgin in Florentine pictures meeting the beautiful, terrible Angel of the Annunciation, she all heaped upon the ground, her slack mouth opening and closing soundlessly.

Then Honey, possessed by some personal devil, darted forward spreading his billowing white sleeves like wings, emitting a high, piercing scream, a spectre, a madman, a vampire.

At last, from the oblong hole of her mouth, came a wild, animal shriek, taking up and fearfully intensifying his own cry; and her withered grey hands clutched at the air and she pitched forward on her face, twitching, convulsive. The flame died. There was no sound but that of the faint movement of the door as it swung to and fro on creaking hinges.

'Why,' asked Morris, whose tongue had gone dry and useless and difficult to manage as chamois leather, 'did you do that?'

'I wanted to see what would happen,' said Honeybuzzard in the voice of an adult pointing out an obvious fact to a dull child. 'I wanted to pull her string.'

Morris felt for his matches and stumbled forward.

'We must try to get help for her, we must fetch a doctor –'

Honey caught at him and pulled him to the door.

'Don't be a fool, Morris; we must go home at once. Now.'

'Home!'

'Come on, quick.'

'But we can't leave her here. Oh, my God, the poor bitch, she may be dying –'

'Come on, you fool!'

The small, hard hands dragged him, protesting feebly, shaken, weak, up the area stairs. The night closed over their heads as if they had jumped into a pond, the silent, enveloping night. Morris gulped down the fresh air, gasping.

'But, you see, I know her! She works in the café and has this warm heart and she is always singing these songs –' His voice broke, he could not think. Inside his head, she went on gathering lilacs in an eternal springtime.

'If she knows you, how can we do anything that might involve the police; do you want to go to prison?'

'But we won't be involving the police!'

They stood for a moment staring at one another, like lovers whose eyes lock in the first moment of ecstatic recognition and think they will never stop looking at each other. Then a muscle moved in Honeybuzzard's cheek and he grasped at Morris's shoulders with a quick, violent movement and flung him bodily against the area railings and his limbs cracked and spread against the jarring metal. Morris spreadeagled for a moment, the breath all knocked out of him; then slid slowly to the ground. Honey sank down on top of him, covering him, holding him down with the weight of his body.

'Doctors fetch policemen, you silly,' he said, almost tenderly, his mouth wet and passionate at Morris's ear. As his mouth closed, he dug his little, sharp, predatory teeth into the soft flesh of the ear-lobe and Morris's eyes closed in a sharp spasm of pain

But the sharp salty pain of the bite went through him and roused him; he gathered unexpected reserves of strength, co-ordinated legs and arms and flung Honey's relaxed weight aside. He bolted down the road.

He made dizzily for a call-box, a dim beacon at the end of the street; he could think, now, only of the need to get help to the woman in the basement and his legs carried him without his mind helping, helter-skelter, with what seemed to him great speed. But before he had gone more than ten yards, Honey was on to him again, jumping him from behind, winding endless steel, monkey arms around his throat.

The cold, hard pavement came crashing up in Morris's face. They rolled, struggling, into the gutter. Morris groped for the other's white face to smash it, obliterate it, shatter it to bone and blood against the sharp edge of the paving stone but it started this way and that; he could not get hold of it.

For an enormous moment, Honey was beneath him and they lay breast to breast, swallowing each other's breath; then, as Morris raised his arms to strike down, Honey somehow twisted free and there was a blinding, jangling pain and Morris crunched up, moaning, into an embryonic ball of pain, clutching his belly, and his eyes filled with a red pain, and when his vision cleared Honey knelt with a knee in his chest and a knife in his hand.

'Don't let me have to kill you, darling,' said Honey. His voice was high, taut and tight.

'This isn't real,' thought Morris. 'I am dreaming. I wonder why I'm dreaming that he's chosen to call me "darling" again. He was fascinated by the little, murderous point of the knife. If he was dreaming, then he was dreaming of a knife, not of the inevitable fact that the knife might be his own death but of the knife itself. The same little point now pricking at his throat had once ripped up the soft flesh of the girl Ghislaine. He knew or thought he knew that it was the same knife. He had never seen it before but he had been curious to see it. He knew he was dreaming when he realized how silly it was that such a little bit of metal should have so much power in it.

'Don't,' repeated Honey. His hair hung over his face in a wedding-veil; he shone with a bridal radiance. His voice sang like the wind in telegraph wires.

'Don't, my darling one!'

And then a discarded newspaper blown on a dark little slapstick breeze blotted out Morris's face and everything vanished but the newspaper, and that was real enough. For a moment, he honestly thought it had killed him and he was dead; then, choking with a reek of fried potatoes and vinegar, coughing, swearing, he tore at the greasy, adhesive, ludicrous thing and felt himself free of the clutch of Honeybuzzard's thighs as the frozen tenseness of the other's flesh melted. There was a click of metal against stone and a gasp; and the beginnings of a great paroxysm of Honey's laughter.

After a few minutes, Morris got the newspaper from his eyes and mouth and threw it down in the gutter beside him. Honey sat on the bottom step of a flight of stone stairs leading up to a blind-eyed, desolate mansion with his head between his hands, laughing and laughing. Morris cautiously tested each aching muscle before rising slowly to his feet. He picked up a knife, which lay on the kerb, and limped over to Honeybuzzard.

'This belongs to you, I think.' He dropped down the knife. A loosened tooth filled his mouth with blood and he spat and found that he was retching. He caught, reeling, at Honey's outstretched hand and slumped down on the step beside him.

'Oh, Morris, what a marvellous anti-climax. What fools we are. Oh, my God, Stan and Olly – Stan and Olly.' He was still murmurous with laughter, shaking his head from side to side.

'Take me home, Honey. I think I might pass out and what would you do then?'

'Oh, poor Morris.'

Supporting all the other's weight, Honeybuzzard led Morris slowly, gently, tenderly to the van. There was a bloody gash on Morris's forehead and a rent in his corduroy jacket and nameless dark stains on his back and trousers. Ripped frills dangled dejectedly from Honey's dandified shirt and there were the beginnings of green and purple bruises down the side of his face. But Honey had regained all his self-possession and he still, from time to time, giggled quietly to himself as he dragged Morris's sick shell along the road.

'What a good thing,' he said comfortably, 'that all this took place in such a twilight zone, where no one comes any more.'

A marauding cat leapt down into an area and dislodged a dustbin lid with Wagnerian echoes that crashed, in Morris's ears, around the very stars, all tiny and flowery and brilliant in the clear, light sky where there was a great, full, silent, smiling moon.

'Look at the moon. A harvest moon, a Mediterranean moon. There should be a brown man playing a guitar and girls with roses in their hair and naked breasts.'

'We ought to do something about the old lady,' Morris said mechanically, through blood.

'We must get you to bed, though, first. You are in a state, aren't you? And we'll think about what to do in the morning.'

He loaded Morris, who hardly seemed capable of moving without aid, into the van. They drove slowly, sedately to the shop. As they politely stopped for a red traffic light, all alone on the road, Morris roused sufficiently to say: 'But we ought to do something about her now.'

'Do be quiet, please.' The voice sharpened.

'I can't, I mustn't. We ought to get a doctor to her –'

'Be quiet before I lose my temper.'

'We might have killed her. I think she was dead. Honey, I think she was dead –'

Half-hysterical, he caught at Honey's arm and the van rocked and skidded. Honey pushed him off.

'For God's sake be quiet!' He struck him a blow across the face. Morris's nose dripped blood. After that, he was quiet.

10

In the shop, Honeybuzzard crumbled four sedatives from a small, brown bottle into a mug of black coffee and poured it down Morris's throat. The scalding liquid ran down Morris's chin and splashed on his filthy shirt; he drank hardly any of it. Honey swore and crumbled two more sedatives into the coffee that remained, forcing Morris's head back so that somehow he got it all down. He mumbled and tried to move his head aside but Honey was too strong for him. Honey dragged him into the workroom, pitched him on to the floor and bundled a blanket roughly under his head.

'Go to sleep, my pretty dear.'

Morris suddenly half rose up and caught at Honeybuzzard's ankle as he went towards the door.

'We did something dreadful –'

Honey kicked him fiercely in the chest with the stabbing high heel of his boot. Morris curled up, coughing. Honey slammed the shaky door. Then he chewed two tablets himself, drinking a great deal of water. He took off his dark glasses, blinking. His eyes were hooded and drooping, perhaps with reaction, but he would only acknowledge to himself that he was unusually tired.

And he staggered with weariness. Emily's cat Tom leapt heavily from the brass bed and came to greet him, purring and rubbing its head against his legs.

'Hello, puss–cat,' he said and yawned. But he stooped down and caressed the cat's head for it, making little, reciprocal mewing noises under his breath. 'Have you caught any mice tonight? Or birds, why don't you catch birds?'

'What were those thumping noises?' said Emily from the black mass of the bed.

'Morris fell down and is suffering from shock.'

'I see,' she said. She had caught the intonation from Morris. Honey stiffened momentarily.

'Emily, I am so tired, so tired.' Naked, he slid between her cool, fresh, clean sheets and sent out a chilly paw towards the warm continent of her body. She clasped him strongly at once. They had been lying in bed for perhaps ten minutes and neither was yet asleep when Morris began to groan. Gently, at first, like the soughing of distant branches, then louder and louder. They heard him more and more distinctly.

'I wish he would not do it,' said Honeybuzzard. Emily rustled beneath the sheets.

'I gave him five sleeping tablets, Emily. He ought to sleep.'

'Christ! Five is enough to put a horse to sleep.'

'I know.'

She sat up in bed to look down at him, questioningly. The bed rattled disapprovingly as though it thought it was too late in the night for jokes. But he was not joking.

'Maybe horses are different,' she said gnomically and lay down again.

The sound continued.

'It is like a storm at sea,' she said.

The sound continued. The shapeless cries of pain formed

themselves into words. Emily sat up again, listening.

'Can't you stay still, woman? Up and down, up and down like a bloody yo-yo!'

'He is unhappy,' she said. Then, listening intently, she said abruptly: 'Oh, my Gawd – did you hear that?'

'He's overtired. And so am I overtired. I want to sleep, so badly; I want to go to sleep!'

There was a low-pitched exclamation followed by sobbing, clear and distinct, coming across the landing to them. In the bronze-coloured city night-light that came through the window, which was curtainless, Emily's still, grave face grew more still, more grave. Her firm mouth set into a determined line.

'But Honey, he is suffering. There is something wrong.'

'So am I suffering. There must be something wrong, he is trying to torment me, he's trying to send me mad by keeping me awake. Die, go on, die, you bastard!' In a frenzy, he threw his pillow at the wall beyond which Morris lay and disappeared entirely under the sheets, head and all.

'Don't be such a silly kid. He's ill. Listen.'

A low, murmurous moaning.

'He ought to be looked after.'

'Go and look after him, then.'

'Shall I?' she asked seriously. A low, sobbing cry came. She flung back the bedclothes and put one long, white leg out of the bed.

'Shall I really go to him, Honey?'

'Yes, oh, yes. Go and do anything you like to him, as long as you quiet him down. So that I can get some sleep.'

'Anything, Honey?'

'Anything, anything.'

She stared at him, a mound under the sheets and blankets. She stared gravely, reflectively.

'Anything,' she repeated to herself.

'Go on, get out ! Shut him up for me, if you love me!'

The expression on her face was quite unguessable but he could not see it. She went to Morris immediately, closing the bedroom door and the workroom door softly behind her.

Morris had struggled clear of the coverings and lay on his face, on the splintering floorboards, half-conscious, half-delirious, weeping uncontrollably. She drew the blankets round him again and made a snug, woollen nest for him; then pulled his head on to her breast, rocking with him in the rhythm of his distress, whispering, 'There, there,' and 'Never mind, everything's all right,' and 'Hush, hush, baby, hush,' in the way she comforted her small sister Teresa or any of her other brothers and sisters over a broken toy or a cut knee. By degrees, he grew quieter and at last lay quite still against her, quite awake, and for the first time perceiving with surprise her bare breasts. He put out a hand, tentatively covering her left nipple.

'It's all right,' she said. 'It's only Emily.' As if it was quite natural that he, clothed, and she, nude, should be lying on the floor of his workroom in the middle of the night.

'Oh, yes,' he said.

'What was the matter? You were ever so upset.'

He tried to speak but could not and shook his head despairingly. The tears ran again. She cradled him more firmly, yet more gently, and put her cheek against his hair.

'Morris, Morris,' she said. 'You were crying so loudly in your sleep and you said you had killed your mother and you were crying so loudly, and I had to come to you.'

He pressed his face between her breasts, where it was moist and dark, and shivered. Somewhere outside a church tower clock struck three and a cock in a back-garden henrun crowed in the idiot middle of the night.

'When I was a little boy,' he said, after a long time, 'I was alone in a room one night, a room in a hotel, with a Bible on the khaki linen cover of the cupboard by the bed, which had a white chamber-pot in its belly, and the sheets were very coarse. I was counting the weft and warp of these sheets by the light of the central bulb, there was only one light, in the middle of the room, and I was counting the threads in the sheets because I couldn't think of anything else to do. And then there were footsteps and they seemed, somehow, agonized. And a voice whining with the speed of the running.'

'Yes,' said Emily gently, stroking his face.

'They went by on a curve of sound under my window and the night gobbled them all up. And after a time there followed them the sound of singing, a great, noisy, singing voice. Outside. Why am I telling you all this?'

'How should I know, poor Morris? But go on, if you want. If it makes you feel better.' With the wounding, impersonal fire of charity which is translated in the fumbling prose of the modernized New Testament as 'love', she passed her hands over his battered body.

'And the singing voice went quickly and had no footsteps with it, which frightened me, and it was going after the footsteps, I knew it. I was too scared to even hide between the sheets. I badly wanted to look out of the window and might have got up enough courage to do it, at last, but there was that black curtaining at the window, too stiff for me to put aside. Anyway, I didn't try. Then there was a hoarse breathing at the door, like a wolf, or as I imagine a wolf's breath might sound if you got up close to it. Rusty, like rusty iron, and the breath itself, I remember thinking, would smell like the taste of pennies.'

'And how old were you then, poor baby?' The term was not an endearment, it merely referred to his small, scared self in the years-ago room.

'Seven, I think. Yes, probably seven. I thought the breathing was my mother's breathing. And I associated it, in some way, with the footsteps and the voice and I knew the breathing was my mother's breathing and there was another breathing going out when her breath came in, two of them, sawing away. And the door began to shake. Later, when I grew up and thought about it, I knew they were . . . making love, but that's not right, there was no love, they were coupling, I suppose . . . anyway, they were doing it upright, against the door. My mother and someone. And then all the lights went out because a bomb had dropped and bed and sheets and bulb and room and door and breathing all vanished and I was on my own and the world had fallen on my head.'

'And were you buried for a long time?'

'For a time. Not for long. And you see, I never saw my mother again, if it was my mother breathing. But I am sure it was my mother, breathing. But she was gone. I don't know if she was dead or if she took it as an excuse to get rid of me. I was a bit of a nuisance, you see, with a war on. But they never found a body that answered to hers. Still, they found a lot of bodies nobody could identify. They buried one of them for my mother. But it may not have been her. I don't know.'

'I don't remember the war at all.'

'Oh, no. You're too young.'

'I am twenty. Not all that young. Some women are married with kids −' she stopped short.

'Young,' he said. He cuddled closer to her, taking soft, greedy, toothless bites at her breasts and shoulders, as if there was nourishment to be got from them. A draught blew in under the door and she wrapped herself round him, warm and cosy as a sheepskin rug.

'It can't have been your mother tonight, then, can it?' she

suggested. 'Not if you remember all this? It seemed to me she must have been killed.'

'But I don't remember that. I only remember that it was likely she was killed but not certain. And this poor old woman — I think we frightened her to death, Emily.'

His voice began to rise again. 'That was why I was telling you all this, because I was never sure she was dead.'

'Softly, now, softly. . . .'

'My mother would have been a poor old woman just like that, by now, all worn out and faceless, and it must have been because of my mother that I used to like her so much when she sang to me in the restaurant. She used to sing how the boy she loved was up in the gallery, waving his handkerchee, and other music-hall songs.'

He began to moan once more, and she, out of the mindless instinct of charity, began softly to caress him because she could think of no other way of making him forget his private horrors for a little while. He resisted her strongly at first but he was weak and ill and she soon overcame him, for her desire to put him away somewhere safely was very great. They strained and wrestled together for a few minutes and then it was all over and all his strength was quite gone. He went to sleep with his arms round her, breathing deeply and evenly.

Emily did not sleep. She lay wide-eyed and motionless while the sky darkened as the moon went down. She listened to the silly cock, crowing at intervals throughout the night. She was not, precisely, thinking; rather, she was rearranging the cumbersome furniture of her mind. The house was so still she could hear the old timbers settling and shifting against one another, hear the liquid gurgle of the water in the cistern like the noise in an old man's guts, hear the faint night sounds of the city's scanty traffic coming in through the ill-fitting window. She grew stiff and cramped but would not move for fear of waking Morris.

Her cat at last succeeded in pushing open the workroom door with its domed forehead and came to where she lay. She was glad to see it and pleased that it would not go to sleep without her, for she felt as lonely as it was possible for her to feel. After purring for a few minutes because it had found her, it curled up and went to sleep on her feet; she was grateful for the warmth. Presently the light grew soft and violet. Dawn was coming. Morris stirred and awoke, drowsy and clinging but in his right mind. She was surprised how chilly and stiff all her muscles were.

'Do you want a cup of tea?' she asked.

'No, thanks. No. I think I'd better be going home, really. Is the night really over?'

'Just about. Do you want to go back to your wife?'

'I want to go home.' But it was not home. Never mind, it will do. He wanted to be surrounded by his own things, to be cosy. . . . Perhaps Edna would be cosy.

Emily wrapped a blanket around herself in a pink toga and stood up. She looked Roman, irreproachable, unapproachable. He remembered he had talked to her a great deal but could not recall a single thing he had told her. It was as if he had dropped pebbles down a deep well and they had vanished without trace. Had he, or hadn't he, entered her? And had she, or hadn't she, coiled her legs around him? But when he saw her silent, serious, Lucretia face turned to him, he could not believe it even as a possibility.

'Are you all right enough to go home, though. That's a question.' She bent and took hold of his hand, felt first his pulse and then his forehead, in a very competent way, while he lay, hardly stirring.

'Your pulse is steady and your forehead cool. Don't lie there malingering. Upsy daisy.'

He let her upsy daisy him and held on to her until a fit of mild giddiness passed.

'You aren't half dirty,' she said with distaste. 'I should have a good clean-up when you get home, if I were you.'

She brushed at a crusted patch of dirt on the sleeve of his jacket, making disapproving clicking noises with her tongue against her teeth.

'Emily,' he asked, consumed with curiosity as she brushed and straightened his clothing. 'Last night. Did I imagine it or did we –'

'I did,' she said briskly. 'Can you manage the stairs?'

'I suppose so.'

'Cheerio, then.'

She picked up her cat, who had been winding about her legs all this time, and went out of the room. He heard the water running in the kitchen. She must be washing – washing him out of herself. He thought, with a certain sense of elation: 'Well, at least I have been unfaithful to my wife after all this time!'

The long walk home was more difficult than he thought it would be. His feet kept slipping and sliding and a recurring giddiness made him pause frequently and breathe in the crisp, early air that was like biting into sharp, green apples, Sturmer pippins or Granny Smiths.

'How will Edna ever know I slept with Honeybuzzard's girl, when Emily is so silent?' he thought, and the thought kept him going for a while.

It was, after all, something of an achievement to have slept with Honey's girl. Although unfortunately he could recall no more of the act than a moment of perfect peace and security when he was tucked up inside her. What had been done was done, though; but he would not really care if he never touched her again. He had never, he realized, wanted Emily for her own sake; and he did not want her, now.

Then he felt so dizzy that he had to sit down on the kerb and a clean working man with a snap-tin bulging his jacket against his large thigh sneered at him disgustedly for a hungover beatnik left over from a long night's party and he himself on such a righteous way to some early-morning shift. Morris felt ashamed. When he was a little recovered, he drew himself up and ran fingers through the brightening morning. He thought his feet made hopeful noises, a proud little pattering tattoo, drums for a regiment sorely battle-scarred yet undefeated, which cheered him. So he crept homeward to the sound of his invisible, hypothetical fifes and drums.

Meanwhile, Emily having washed herself and put on clean underwear and her skirt and sweater because of the chill in the morning, made a pot of tea and drank two cups. She set down a saucer of tinned cat food for Tom. Tom quivered on the table with scarcely controllable excitement while she opened the tin and spooned out the meat. She made one or two attempts to shoo him on to the floor, for she did not think that cats should be allowed on tables where food was prepared for human beings, but he leapt back so relentlessly that suddenly she could not manage to make the effort to keep him away. She held the table edge for a moment and then her face twitched and she reached the sink in time to vomit into the washing-up bowl.

After sitting down for a little, she rinsed out the bowl with hot water and disinfectant and poured out another cup of tea. But vomited the tea, all thin and curdled, at once. She looked in the mirror; her cheeks were pale. She pressed both hands against her stomach, feeling the soft flesh – then exclaimed sharply: 'Oh, don't be such a stupid bitch!'

She could not keep still but moved restlessly about the kitchen, picking things up and putting them down. Once she said, 'Holy Mary, Mother of God, please – don't make me,' and then shook her head in sad self-reprimand for her superstition.

Her cat, sides stuffed out with breakfast, stretched and yawned and sent its pink tongue swiftly over its whiskers, chasing last crumbs. Then it rolled over on its back and began a comprehensive morning toilet, energetically cleaning tail and hind legs and chest and finally righting itself and rubbing cheeks and ears with a cunning curved paw. It did Emily good to see her cat so brisk and businesslike and preoccupied; she leant against the table and watched him.

It was now beginning to be entirely morning. She went downstairs to the lavatory through the shop. Over the road, the laundry was beginning to hum, already. From a huge van drawn up outside the butcher's, two men in bloody overalls hurled great joints of meat, red sides of beef and amber-rinded pork and white legs of lamb and rosy shoulders of mutton into the waiting arms of the butcher, who stood on the pavement in his filthy blue apron and bloodstained straw boater, around which the flies already buzzed.

And, already, there was someone in the street, a tiny little girl standing outside the window, looking in at the dress of flamingo satin. She wore a shiny black raincoat that came down to the middle of her blue-jeaned thighs, and on the back of her yellow head was a peaked, shiny, black oilskin cap such as engine drivers wear. Emily wanted the cap for Honey and then switched off the idea of Honey. For a moment, Emily thought the girl was very beautiful and very young, perhaps only thirteen or fourteen. But then she moved and the light fell on her face.

There was the healed scar of a great wound down one side of her face. The whole cheek was a mass of corrugated white flesh, like a bowl of blancmange a child has played with and not eaten. Through this devastation ran a deep central trough that went right down her throat under the collar of her coat. Grainy fragments of cosmetics were lodged in the crevices and crannies of the shattered face, whitewash slapped on a crumbling wall. But the other half of the face was fresh and young and smooth and warm as fruit in the sunlight. The two sides of the moon juxtaposed.

She seemed preparing to wait outside the shop for a long time. As Emily watched her, the girl put a cigarette in her mouth and lit it; she blew a perfect smoke-ring and quickly put her finger through it before it dissolved. She laughed. When she laughed, half her face was that of a happy baby and the other half, crinkled up, did not look like a face at all. Emily, swallowing to keep down a return of nausea, went on to the lavatory.

She stayed there a long time, hoping the girl would go away, but when she returned, the girl was still only stubbing out her cigarette, stretching and yawning. Emily meant to pass straight through the shop and go upstairs but found she could not. She wanted to stay and watch the girl, see what she would do and who she waited for, find out why she stood out there, with her Hallowe'en mask face, although she was strangely and unreasoningly afraid of her.

The girl lit another cigarette. Emily noticed that the girl's hands were brown with nicotine stains. Emily put her own cold hands up the sleeves of her sweater to warm them, for she was very cold, and glanced around the familiar interior. She felt chilled and apprehensive, unlike herself. 'It must be something to do with being sick like that.' But she looked at the stuffed carp, the naked boy with the hat on his head, the Abbotsford chair, the horned gramophone, as if imploring the protection of these inanimate things against the spectre with the exploded beauty who waited outside.

The scarred girl stepped out on to the roadway to peer up at the upstairs window to see if she could spy any sign of life inside. Now she came close to the shop window and peered in, screwing up her eyes. Emily moved uneasily and the girl saw the movement; she dropped her cigarette and leapt to life, beating furiously at the door with her small fists, shaking it and crying: 'Let me in! Let me in!' Her voice was shrill and clear. Emily thought how big her eyes were, and how brown.

Shrugging, Emily stepped over the horned gramophone to unlock the door. She felt she was being very brave but, also, that there was nothing else she could do.

11

Rattling milk bottles on a float drowned the shouting of the small birds in the copper beech tree as Morris went into his house and dragged himself up the steep stairs, clinging to the mahogany stair rail, which was sticky from some child's unwashed fingers. His legs were still soft and wobbling. Fumbling before his own front door, he dropped his key and when he stooped to pick it up all the blood in his body surged at once into his head, swirling away like a storm at sea. He nearly fell on his face. He straightened himself against the doorpost and closed his eyes. A blood-coloured carousel whirled behind his eyelids; he waited patiently for it to grind to a standstill, savouring the curious metallic taste in his mouth.

'The walk has exhausted me,' he thought.

He sat on a stool in the kitchen for ten minutes, smoking a number of foul-tasting cigarettes. Then he blundered into the bedroom to put himself to bed. The curtains were still drawn across the open window; they slowly swelled, slowly collapsed with the movements of the wind and the room was full of gently shifting shadows.

There was a sweetish smell of spilled powder around the

dressing-table where the wind stirred the glinting starling's nest of Edna's shed hairpins beside a splayed brush and a gap-toothed comb. Over a chairback hung a ghostly white nylon slip, in softly rippling motion, and the twin peaks of a discarded white brassiere stuck up through stockings puddled on the seat. Morris dreamily recollected that it was Saturday morning and Edna would still be catching up on her week of hard work and worried nights. He swayed towards the bed.

The striped Indian coverlet was humped over two forms. Slowly, dreamily, he made out two profiles flat against the pillows, both pointing the same way, like heads in a child's drawing. The head of another man lay on the pillow where his own head ought to be.

The sheet was scrunched down around the other man's pale shoulders and defenceless neck and Morris made out the pink bud of a round boil at the base of the ragged hairline. It was Henry Glass, breathing prickly lungfuls of Edna's flooding brown hair in his harmless sleep. They slept in unison, with a twin rising and falling of the coverlets.

On a first blind impulse of outrage, Morris sprang forward; his feet tangled in Henry Glass's thrown down trousers and the white arms of Henry Glass's flung off shirt wound round his ankles and brought him to a halt. With drunken concentration, Morris worked for what seemed to him a very long time to free himself from Henry Glass's claggy, slimy, snaking clothing, and when at last he kicked them away from him his anger was all gone.

They slept so trustingly, so small, so warm, so snug. Henry Glass's arm over Edna's buttocks, their hair marrying, brown and fair, like milk and coffee poured out together over the pillows, their two soft mouths curved flower-like in tranquillity, their tender eyelids waxen petals of repose. In the cosy pod of the bedclothes, they lay close as peas. Morris listened to the faint music of their shallow breathing.

He tiptoed back to the kitchen. He splashed his face with cold water. The chilly drops seemed to shock him into a sharp-outlined clearness of vision. He saw everything extremely distinct and very small, in brilliant miniature. He felt he could pick up the bed in his two hands, minutely examine its occupants, poke and finger every detail, like Gulliver among the Lilliputians. And his Edna slept so sweetly and so happily, with somebody else.

He cleaned his teeth, his terrible teeth, which hurt him a great deal. The toothbrush was red with blood when he put it down, and he thought: 'I shall really have to go to the dentist's now.' He had a quick foresight of himself in the chair, the man in the white coat investigating his mouth, the water bubbling in the basin beside him, the nurse waiting; it was a memory of the future. He knew that, this time, he was certainly going to go to the dentist, it would all happen. He was, for the first time, sure of something. He brushed his hair, neatly, and rubbed the worst of the mess from his clothes with a tea towel dipped in water. He polished his shoes.

Then he went silently into the living-room and found pen and paper. He wrote very rapidly a few words for Edna. The words marched brisk and black from the pen and arranged themselves in neat ranks on the page; he must have had them formulated in his mind for years. He did not need to read the letter through when it was finished.

'I am going away. Be happy. He needs you so much more than I do. Thank you for loving me, although I never deserved it. Morris.'

He propped the note against the sugar bag in the kitchen, where she would be sure to see it, then let himself out of the flat and ran down the stairs he had pulled himself up with such effort a short time before. His weakness had been washed away with the cold water. Brisk and spruce, neat and clean, he began to run.

He ran down the road, faster and faster till he thought he might leave the ground and start flying, so fast was he running, running to get away from the flat and all the rank memories it contained. Edna bending forward, offering to him the ill-cooked food she spent so much time and effort preparing. Edna before the evening mirror, rubbing the greasy cotton-wool over her face. Edna in suds to the elbow wearily scrubbing the ground-in dirt from shirt-collar and cuffs. Edna weeping because she had seen him chatting up some wet-lipped party girl. Edna moaning in a darkened room, stricken with a headache. Edna talking with total incomprehension about painting. Edna opening her legs to Henry Glass out of sheer compassion.

The jig-saw-puzzle piece of Oscar's message clicked into place. Watch out, Morris, or the meek, the suffering, the humble Henry Glass will inherit your neglected wife. And so he had.

But Edna and Henry Glass would be very happy. They would talk for hours of the memory of Mrs Henry Glass and she could release her great well-springs of tenderness and drown him in them and he would just love it. And she would wear Henry Glass's rotten jewellery, and he would put up shelves for her in the kitchen and make her pale wood cupboards and three-legged stools and toys of awesome simplicity for the children they would have together (for they would have lots of children), and he would never dream of letting her go out to work and her cooking would improve (maybe) and she would bake wholemeal loaves and make chutney from windfall apples and they would go out blackberrying, all the family together, laughing among the red and yellow autumn leaves, and she would put on weight.

And this rich tapestry of life would be woven from the spun thread of her compassion.

(Emily, also, the previous night, when the moon had been fat, white, female and mysterious, had opened her legs out of compassion. So was behaving compassionately simply something women did when the moon was full? Edna and Emily, behaving in the same way. . . .

(But it was not the same way, not at all. Edna would think that loving or being in love with Henry Glass would make the act seemly, fitting and moral and, besides, Henry Glass's need was so great and his predicament so tragic. She would overwhelm Henry Glass in tenderness and affection and be comfortable and make a relationship. And if she felt any guilt at betraying her husband, her first husband, it would be a pleasant spice to season the nourishing, plain pudding of her life. It was, then, a compassion bred of or breeding total human involvement.

(And Emily? Hard, cool, impersonal Emily had done what she could to stop him crying and, this morning, dismissed him like a kindergarten teacher, sending him away with her work done. And nothing more to say. Which was the more genuine compassion, Edna's emotional giving of self or Emily's stylized abstraction? Which, in fact, was the best buy from the point of view of the object of either compassion?)

He was deep in his problematical parenthesis when he reached the centre of the town and automatically turned into the cafe for a cup of tea, and, as he sat drinking it, he mentally washed his hands of the problem of compassion and thought about what he was going to do, now. He would go away, really go away, and forget about them all, really forget them all, and find an honest job, glass-blowing or gas-fitting or building roads, somewhere far, far away. Should he go to Israel and work on a kibbutz? But this idea had the smack of one of his fantasies and he was determined that he would, in future, put such fantasies behind him – he would become a citizen of the real world, a world where there was black and there was white but no shadows. He felt as though he was acting as his own midwife at his own rebirth; Morris Gray was being reborn as a new, hard, practical man. When his tea was half-drunk, he heard singing:

'Won't you come home, Bill Bailey, won't you come home . . .'

Edna, mournful, reproachful, floated suddenly in his cup, wearing her white beads which had the appearance of a lot of little skulls. Skulls of their babies, never to be born, only another Morris to be born. Perhaps she really loved him, perhaps bedding with Henry Glass was meant to be only a single gesture, perhaps her heart would break because he was gone . . . she wavered, she dissolved.

Morris trembled because he would not believe that he heard singing.

The Struldbrug, in her grey overall and her grey head-dress and her white apron, all complete, slapped her rag across the table and gave him her warmest and most affectionate leer.

'How's my dearie, this lovely morning?' she asked.

'All the better for seeing you,' he told her. Truthfully, how truthfully. He grinned foolishly. He could not think for joy. The café exploded with joy. He could not help grinning away.

'Have – a cigarette . . .' he dug for the package. He had to give her something, to reward her for being so alive. She giggled and pushed him playfully.

'Get away with you! Me – smoking on duty! They'd give me the sack, one, two, pronto, they would. "OUT!" they'd say!'

He wanted to embrace her to convince himself she was real, snatch at her grey overall, catch her hand, but she made off immediately for another table, singing her little song. He had forgotten until he saw her that he thought he had helped to kill her.

The suddenness of her resurrection was miraculous. Lazarus, she waddled away on her creaking black shoes, moulded over the years to the shape of the horny, corny, nooks and crannies and lumps and bumps and crevices and promontories and fjords of her swollen and time-deformed feet. The grey lisle stockings swagged richly about her ankles. Her back bunched and bent with age and fat and life. She was alive.

Alive.

His heart sprang up lightly, dancing with the plastic oranges on the carboy of orange squash. The hot water splashed from the urns in deliriously joyful fountains. The marzipan petals on the fondant cakes shook out in gay green life. Deep notes of joy rang from the cream horns. The eclairs – eclairissement – burst under the pressure of the sweet white cream of joy. The ham rolls bounded like ecstatic piglets from their Cellophane pens. The soft globes of artificial light crashed down like shooting stars. He thought he would go out of his mind with joy.

He went out into the street, dazed. The street beamed in the arse-end of summer and the women who passed him were beautiful and the men distinguished and even the dogs were interesting.

A fishmonger's window appeared like a vision in Vaughan or Traherne, a transcendental vision of mystical ecstasy. The white slivers of plaice, the corn-gold haddock, the winking shells of cockles and mussels that held deep-sea colours in their blue-black shells, horned prawns in Samurai armour, the smiling fishmonger himself, all held some numinous significance, ideal forms from a universe where dead women walked and the past could run back on itself and there was palpable, tangible joy in the air. All round the slab, the plastic parsley clustered thickly, as if the marble itself were fertile – the marble was magically breaking out with the green grass of Elysium. A boy in a white pinafore glinting with fish-scales spilled a bucket of odourous water from the door in a cascade of diamonds, opals, sapphires, emeralds – what was it, the water of life? It wetted Morris's trousers but he did not care.

From the doorway, an aged Didekei woman with a sepia-wash face and whining, gravy-coloured eyes tried to sell him a bunch of dahlias, pretty little heads on stalks, all deep red and velvety and speckled. First he pushed past; then spun around and emptied his pockets of change to buy four bunches from her crammed basket and she, in an orgy of gratitude, pushed handfuls of maidenhair fern into his arms. He went on flowering like a harvest festival.

At first he thought he would take them to the café and give them to the Struldbrug; but that would be too ostentatious. Next, should he send them to Edna, for services rendered? But she was in bed with Henry Glass; perhaps at this very moment stirring awake with him, turning to him with a fresh awakening of desire. So the debt was cancelled. No flowers for Edna. So he would take them to the shop and give them to Emily, because he must go to the shop, anyway, and tell her he had not killed the little old lady at all and the poor alcoholic old lady did not even remember what had happened or had dismissed it all as a drink-nightmare.

Besides, he would have to say good-bye to Honey. He wanted to say good-bye to Honey, he realized, though he remembered enough of the previous night (which began, now, to seem like nothing but a nightmare to himself) to know it would be difficult. But he felt happy enough to cope with anything.

He thought he had never been so happy. Even the sunlight was trying to please him by burning, now, with diminished strength. The sky might be dark blue and gold but the trees were yellowing and there were fur-trimmed coats for ladies in the shop windows and the dresses the girls wore drooped wearily as if they had been overworked, and all the bare, brown arms were beginning to have a cindery look, from burning all through the summer. Soon the sky would cloud over for good and it would be fairly autumn. He thought he would buy some new clothes, for the autumn, and give his green jacket away to a tramp. And, perhaps, shave his beard, for the travelling.

There was no one in the front part of the shop although the door was open. As he moved into the dark interior, he saw there was a great deal of smoke seeping in through the half-open back door and, when he pulled it open, a black wall of smoke fell forward and hit him in the face and made his eyes water and brought on a tremendous fit of coughing.

When he could see again, and had his handkerchief protectively over his mouth, he saw that Emily knelt in the backyard before a large fire in a metal dustbin from which came streamers of pale orange flame that almost licked her blackened face, so closely did she lean over it, and a theatrical amount of smoke. Witch-like, she poked at her cauldron with a stick and, as he watched, flung on an armful of vivid coloured rags, green, scarlet and yellow, that danced in the air for a second as on a washday line, and then swooped down to destruction. A wave of smoke surged up and she vanished inside it.

When this cleared, she was standing up, rubbing her streaming eyes with filthy knuckles. Her hair stuck out in a demented Struwwelpeter mop, her clothes were as smeared and smutty as her face, her arms.

'Oh,' she said, without surprise. 'It's you. What do you want?'

He pushed forward the flowers, wordlessly. She eyed them for a moment without any expression on her face and then shrugged and pushed past him into the house. He followed her up the stairs and into Honeybuzzard's room. The ground had fallen away under him. What next, my God, what next?

The bedroom was a scene of total devastation. The corset advertisements were ripped and torn from the walls and so were all the photographs and drawings. The calceolaria was wrenched out of its pot and lay on its side on the windowsill, with its roots in a bear-trap of clotted earth. Broken in half, the bust of Queen Victoria rolled in the grate. Upended drawers covered the bed with Honey's grotesque finery. Emily filled her arms with clothing and turned to go downstairs again.

'What happened to the foetus?' he asked. It was gone from the windowsill.

'I flushed it down the lavatory,' she said harshly. 'It made me sick. Let me by.'

He followed her back down the stairs, shedding tufts of maidenhair fern all the way. In the backyard, she stuffed two frilled shirts and a string vest into the dustbin and stirred the fire.

'What are you doing, Emily?' he asked.

'Burning him, the bastard. Burning him all up.' Into the fire went a tee-shirt with a picture of Ludwig von Beethoven on the front of it. She struck Beethoven vindictively in the face with her stick and he crumbled in black ashes.

'Go and put those things in the sink,' she ordered, nodding at his flowers. 'Did you get them off the gipsies?'

'Yes.'

'They pinch all the flowers they sell out of graveyards. Go and put them in the sink.'

He would rather have thrown a valedictory bunch on the pyre of Honey's clothes. But she spoke so firmly he went to the kitchen and put the poor dahlias and what remained of the maidenhair fern into the washing-up bowl, which he filled with water. Then he put the kettle on, in order to make Emily some tea, which he hoped might soothe her. While he waited for the kettle to boil, she came and went up and down the stairs several times and the pillar of smoke continued to ascend outside the window. When the tea was made, he caught her on the landing and pushed a cup of tea into her hand.

'But I've not finished yet,' she protested. There was a different quality about her, as if the Emily he had known, clean, precise, good Emily, were sleeping inside and this destructive, mindless, vindictive machine had taken over. He badly wanted her to drink the tea, to prove that she was still human.

'Drink this up and it will refresh you,' he pleaded.

'I'm not going to stop till I've got rid of every shred of him.' Flat and lifeless, she spoke.

'Just rest for a moment and drink up this nice tea.'

To his inexpressible relief, she took a tentative sip and finally allowed herself to be led into the kitchen and settled on a chair.

'What is the matter, now, Emily?'

She stared at him blankly from her blackamoor face.

'He's gone. A girl came for him this morning.'

'A girl?' Morris had a premonition of horror. 'What sort of girl?'

'Little and fair, with a great, big scar. There isn't enough sugar in my tea.'

He spooned more sugar for her and stirred the cup. She drank; the words came more freely.

'This girl came in and she told me things about him. How he aborted her with a rusty knitting needle in here, on this table −' she put her hand firmly on the table, as if to exorcise it −' and she went bad inside and can't have babies.'

'That was a lie,' said Morris drearily.

'Well, I didn't believe that, as a matter of fact. Not when I thought about it; I thought it was a bit much, you know.' The only sign of her distress was her dirtiness and untidiness, now that her speech was less strained and staccato. Her movements were as deliberate as ever, her face as calm. She bit at her fingernails; then made a little shudder as she saw how dirty they were. 'She talked ever so funny, in this high, sad, mad, little voice and she went on and on and on. All these horrible things she said he'd done to her and she said he would do them to me, sooner or later. And she showed me these photographs of him and her –'

'Oh, God –'

'Oh' she shrugged. 'There was nothing there I hadn't seen before.'

'Oh.'

'I knew Honey was the sort who – you know? – liked to show you what he could do. But she was so pretty in them, she had such a pretty face. And she kept pushing her face, her horrible face, all scarred and torn, into mine and said he would cut me up like that if I did anything he didn't like. Like going to bed with anyone else. Or getting pregnant. And that upset me a bit, in the circumstances.'

She drank more of her tea, composedly. Morris reached out a gentle hand and placed it on her arm. She ignored him.

'Then she made me kiss her, on the scar. She said: "Kiss it, kiss it, kiss it," and she came right up close to me. Then Honey came in and she ran off away from me as if she'd forgotten all about me and lay down in front of him. Right on the floor. It was –' she fumbled for a word, found a shockingly inadequate one –' disconcerting. She said: "I've learned my lesson, I can't live without you, you are my master, do what you like with me." That's exactly what she said, I remember every word. "You are my master." And he just laughed. It upset me, he just laughed and then he put on that soppy cap with the stripes and went. Just like that. He told me to take care of myself and went. And he didn't say where he would be going or if he would be back, he just took her hand and they got into the van and drove off together. Just like that.'

She finished her tea and poured more. Morris said awkwardly: 'And so you started burning everything, did you?'

She gestured emphatically with her free hand.

'Oh, it wasn't that I was burning him out for. Only, I went to the doctor's afterwards and the rotten bastard's got me in the family way.'

There was a long silence, during which she drank her second cup of tea.

'Are you sure?' Morris's voice was hoarse and rough.

'Well, I thought I probably was. That was why I didn't bother to do anything before we had it last night, I thought, "Oh, well, why bother." And the doctor says I'm three months gone and ought to be having free milk and that. He felt right up me with a big rubber glove and it's there, all right. It was very humiliating, the glove,' she added unexpectedly. 'Still, that's how it is and I can't very well sue the rubber goods shop, can I?'

Morris felt very cold and quite empty, as though his guts had been siphoned out. All the tinsel and fairy lights were stripped from the Christmas tree of the bright, hopeful morning and he gazed at the bare boughs in a chilly wind and wondered where the glitter had gone. And what would happen now the woman, the fiend woman from the monster magazines, had returned? And had taken away Honey? And was that the hardest to bear, that Honey was gone?

'I wish she were dead,' he said vehemently.

'It's not her fault,' said Emily. 'If someone did that to me, I'd go a bit round the bend, too.'

'Did what?'

'Cut me up. Honey did it to her, didn't he?'

'Yes. Did she tell you?'

'No. I guessed. I'm not a fool, you know. It's all over with Honey, now, as far as I'm concerned. He could whistle for me for ever but I wouldn't come.'

'But you say you're pregnant –'

'That's my affair, isn't it?' Her nigger-minstrel mouth, all pink and rubbery among the soot, hardened to a firm, narrow line. 'It's inside *me*, not inside him, isn't it?'

A little knob of flesh, a rosebud, a strawberry, scarcely formed, growing in the rich soil of her belly. Honey's child.

'Do you want an abortion?' He spoke more barely and cruelly than he intended. She stiffened as if he had slapped her.

'No, I do not ! I called my piper, so I'll pay for my tune, thank you very much.'

'But Emily –'

'If it hadn't been him, it would have been somebody else, sooner or later. So it can be sooner and I'll have my baby.'

Peasant fatalism. Or the few remains of the family Catholicism she had consciously denied. Or her own stubborn simplicity that said you can't take a life that has been given you, even when it is hardly formed, no more than a finned tadpole swimming in a bag of water under your striped sweater. She was very matter of fact and cool; Morris was blank and dazed but she was on an even keel again. She looked inside the teapot to see if there was more tea. There was not. She replaced the lid with a sigh.

'Ooh, I felt awful when I got back from the doctors,' she said. 'You keep on hoping you're wrong, you know, up till the last minute. I wasn't half angry with Honey, I wanted to smash all his rotten rubbish up. I don't know what came over me. I feel ashamed of myself, now, 'cos it's not his fault really. It's just the way things are. And I don't love him any more. I mean, wouldn't it have been dreadful if I still loved him?'

As if to demonstrate that she was entirely herself again, she went to the sink, carefully put the bowl of flowers on the draining board and began to scrub her arms.

'I could do with a bath,' she said.

'Did he leave me a message?'

'Who, Honey? 'Course not – why should he? He wasn't,' she said gently, 'feeling very friendly to you last night, you know. Ooh, he is a bastard. Thank God I've finished with him.'

'You shouldn't have let him go alone!'

'What?'

'There's something wrong with him, he needs help. He oughtn't to go with Ghislaine, I know it. He –'

'He's not a kid. What he does is his own business and if he wants to go off with that mad bitch, then it's up to him, isn't it.'

'But I don't know what he might do with her. Oh, God, if only I knew. . . . He's always seemed so essential to me, like a limb. You can't call your hand a friend, it's just there. And you don't bother to ask it why it does things – picks things up, puts them down. And he was like my hand that belonged to me but I never understood how it functioned.'

He was talking aloud to himself, alone in the cold. But Emily shot him a speculative and curious look from under her heavily marked eyebrows. The kitchen filled with the smell of Lifebuoy toilet soap. She took off her sweater and washed her armpits. Morris went rambling on to himself.

'I never thought about him, he was always there. Until last night, last night . . .'

'There's one thing,' she said. 'If he doesn't come back soon, I'm going out to find him.'

'Why? But you said –'

'I'm just going to find him. I want some money. I don't see why he shouldn't give me some money to get back to London with. I haven't got any.'

'Neither have I.'

'Well, then. I'm going back to London tonight, to my Mum and Dad, and Honey's going to pay my fare. He ought to. He brought me down here, didn't he?'

She towelled herself and vanished to change her dress. She returned pink and combed. He had never seen her look so clean. She dazzled his eyes. It was a transformation. She took eggs from the cupboard.

'We'll have a bite to eat. Gawd, I'm ever so hungry. It's the kid, I couldn't keep nothing down this morning. And I'm starving, now.' She cracked eggs, cut bread, took out butter, broke off and chewed a bit of crust hungrily. She shook the dahlias from the washing-up bowl. 'For me, are they?'

'I suppose so.' He had been happy when he bought them.

'Ta,' she said and directed the full force of her sun-on-water smile, her special smile, into his eyes. It was only the second time she had smiled this smile for him.

12

He went to get cigarettes from the tobacconist's next door but there was a blue blind on the door and a notice, 'closed'. The dummy cigarette packets were all disarrayed. He went to a grocer's he sometimes used, a hundred yards away.

'How is what's-his-name up the road?'

The grocer left off slicing bacon and shook his head sadly.

'Gone, at last. Blessed release, though *she* took it badly, of course. Sudden, really – without warning; though you might have seen it, being so close.'

'But I was in there yesterday – when did he go?'

'Last night. They took him to the undertaker's this morning. They tidy them away, these days. Not like in the old days. I remember my father, poor old chap, stuck in the front room for five days – and it was only a two-up, two-down house, and six of us kids. And such a hot summer that year. Hot as this summer. But it's not like in the old days, not with corpses.'

Morris looked at the pink flesh and white fat of the bacon. Human flesh, they say, eats like pig. Cannibals call it long pig.

'What about the wife? She didn't look too good herself.'

'Gone to stay with her sister in Weston till the funeral; she looks proper washed-out, white as a sheet. She'll be the next to go, if she's not careful. It always comes in threes.'

'What does?' asked Morris, bemused.

'Death.' The grocer tidied away a loose crumb or two of cheese upon the counter and asked briskly: 'Now, what can I do you for sir?'

'Oh . . . you do sell cigarettes, don't you? Twenty Woodbines.'

This was why they invented cigarettes, to relax you. Morris had never before, he thought, really needed to smoke, not until now.

Emily set him to work in the shop all the rest of that day, clearing away the things she had torn and broken. She directed him as they scrubbed the walls with soap and warm water to get rid of the shreds that remained of the strange pictures Honey had pasted on them. They took down and put away in drawers the false noses that clustered like bright little toadstools in every place. With a blank face, Emily carried various objects down to the shop and set them up for sale. She took the brocaded hat from the statue of the nude boy and burnt it in the dustbin and Morris recalled that Ghislaine had worn the hat in one of the photographs. But this was the last thing she burned.

She made up the big, brass bed and turned the sheet down and said firmly, arms akimbo, 'Well, I'm never going to sleep in *that* again.' Penitently, she smoothed and folded what few clothes of Honey's she had not committed to flames. She rearranged the tumbled toys she had scattered over the floor into a workmanlike pile but Morris saw that the Ghislaine Jumping Jack was gone. Then she washed her face again and combed her hair again and said accusingly: 'Well, it doesn't look as though he's coming back, does it? Do you know where he is?'

Morris moved uneasily. Last night and the plaster Christ. This morning and Ghislaine inviting Honey to do as he liked. It fitted, it was likely, but it appalled him. Yet he admitted at last, 'I think I might know,' because Emily's eyes were so stern and demanding.

'It is only a chance, mind,' he warned.

'Beggars can't be choosers. We'll go now.'

'No, not now – and, Emily, let me go by myself. I'll explain and get you some money. It is a long way. And it's only a chance.'

'I said, "we'll go", both of us. It's my affair, isn't it, more than yours. I'll pack my things and be ready to go on home afterwards.'

She packed her skirt and sweater, wrapping them in newspaper so that they would not dirty the inside of her duffel bag. She put her toothbrush and the cake of Lifebuoy toilet soap (first wrapping it in her face flannel) in a crimson plastic sponge bag and put this in her duffel bag as well. She also packed a small plastic bag containing some cosmetics and her comb. Her movements had the formal precision of ballet. She removed all traces of her stay from the flat, leaving not a hair nor a lipstick stain behind.

'Right.'

'We must wait until it gets dark.' He could not go there in daylight, even if Honey could. She nodded, accepting this without further question, and drugged her cat with half an aspirin in a saucer of milk.

'I'll leave my stuff here and pick it up afterwards. We won't be long, will we?'

'I don't know,' said Morris. 'Oh, stay here, Emily – they

will be together, if they are there, Honey and Ghislaine.'

'So what?' she said.

So they waited until a portcullis of slate blue cloud hung in the west, ready to fall, and then they walked out together. All raspberry and apricot, blueberry and vanilla, the sky melted softly in soda fountain colours over the city, a huddle of roofs, chimneys, spires and bone-white skyscrapers winking their windows redly on the sunset side, and the sweetness drawn from the green fields on the horizon hung in the warm air. The summer seemed to be saying good-bye to itself, bestowing upon itself this long, golden, poignant, farewell, evening smile.

The muted and elegaic light seemed to be that filling a dead city. It was the light of the city of dream-come-true. Morris felt like his own shadow, moving silently past windows where television sets glowed whitely, bluely; where roses spread in a red, yellow and pink plastic fan in lustre vases; where plaster Alsatian dogs romped between red plush curtains. They saw hardly another walker. A girl in shorts whirled by on a beautiful, young bicycle. A car slid by with cushions on its wheels. That was all.

Emily walked in a disciplined, almost martial stride and her arms swung to the rhythm of her walk. Her sleek hair bounced on her nape and her large breasts moved steadily up and down. She walked as if she had a destination ahead of her of which she was quite sure. It was like walking with a symbol of the norm. Morris felt less shadow-like the more they went on together.

He discovered that he was not afraid. He was too empty to feel afraid either of Ghislaine or of Honeybuzzard's reaction to Emily's visit. They would go together, he and Emily, to the house with the rosaries where he half-guessed, half-knew they would find Honey, and Emily would take her payment due and he, Morris, would take her safe home to her parents' house and then he would be in London. He was a free man, now, and could plan for his future. If there was to be a future, of which he was not completely assured. He remembered that there was something he had to tell Emily. He had forgotten, his memory was going, he had forgotten. . . .

'Emily,' he said. 'I – we . . . the old lady. She's still alive. I saw her, this morning. We didn't kill her.'

He thought she would be glad but she only said rather sarcastically: 'Well, well, whatever next. And I never thought you had killed her, either. Lot of fools.'

He was awed by her stolidity, her resolution. He glanced at her and saw that her mouth had never been so firmly closed, locked and padlocked. He was oddly reminded of the bust of Queen Victoria and thought: 'I don't think I have ever seen Emily laugh.' There was nothing to amuse her in the world. And she had excised Honey from her heart and mind without a second thought, purposefully put him out of doors. Morris did not know that her affections were to let again, but he was impressed by the speed and efficiency with which she had evicted the present tenant. And she was so serene.

The sweet night thickened as if somewhere someone was boiling it up like jam. Now it had reached the stage where a spoonful would set on a saucer. All was still. They stood in last night's deserted street.

'Where are we going?'

'Into one of those houses.'

'Oh.'

She followed him into the hot darkness and, as on the night before, he went up to the roof of the first house and out on to the airy leads, and down into the second house's disordered attics. He found a stub of candle in his pocket. And the doll's head, forgotten, rolling beside his handkerchief and a few pennies in small change. It smiled at him but he no longer wanted it. He dropped it on the floor.

He wondered anxiously in the boarded-up blackness if he had been mistaken. He thought Honey had remembered his own joke and brought Ghislaine to the room where the plaster Christ was nailed down, he was sure of it . . . but there was no sound in the house, no glimmer of any light.

Then, as they crept cautiously down the next flight of stairs, he saw a yellow stain seeping round the edges of the door on the floor below. Candlelight. They must go carefully.

But they did not find Honey there. Instead, they found the room with the folding chairs illuminated by innumerable candles stuck with their own grease to every horizontal surface. The room blazed with light and there was a silence so intense it was almost audible. The air throbbed with the tension of maintaining its own stillness.

The candles were burning low, dribbling wax like running noses, long tears of wax. There was a thick, rich smell of melted tallow. How big the room was, and how high. Every cobweb and crack in the plastering stood out with the clarity of *trompe l'oeil* in the candlelight. Honey must have emptied the cupboard of candles and set a match to every one of them.

A collapsible trestle table had been assembled in the middle of the floor. Morris could not remember where it might have come from. On the table lay a mound, covered with a chequered tablecloth. At each of the four corners of the table burned a candle. Morris became painfully conscious of the beating of his heart.

'Wait here,' he said to Emily in the doorway. She glanced at him disdainfully and went with him to the table. He did not want Emily to see what might be lying under the cover but, as he tried to press her behind him, she reached across and turned the cover down.

Naked, Ghislaine lay on her back with her hands crossed on her breasts, so that her nipples poked between her fingers like the muzzles of inquisitive white mice. Her eyes were shut down with pennies, two on each eyelid, and her mouth gaped open a little. There were deep black fingermarks in her throat. With pity and tenderness, for the first time unmixed with any other feeling, Morris saw how her fingernails were bitten down to the quick and how shadows smoothed out the cratered surface of her cheek and how the chopped tufts of golden hair had grown no farther than an inch or so below her ears and how there was soft, blonde down on the motionless flesh of her stomach.

Emily abruptly went to a corner of the room, where she vomited splashily. She leaned against the wall for a little while, with her arms around her middle, where the baby was, as if to protect it from the sight. Morris covered Ghislaine up again. They stood there and the candles burned away.

After a time, Emily said: 'He did that. Honey.'

'Yes,' said Morris.

'Why?'

'I don't know. He wanted to.'

They found they were speaking very quietly so as not to wake her.

'They will hang Honey or put him away,' Emily said.

Honey, as bright as Lucifer before his fall, gasping to death at the end of a rope or among madmen for the rest of his life, if you could call it a life. For doing what Morris had always wanted but never defined . . . for choking out of Ghislaine her little-girl giggle and stopping the chiming clock (telling half past the hour for Morris, three-quarters past for Honeybuzzard, she made out of the falling syllables of their names, filling up her voracity once and for all by cramming with death the hungry mouth between her thighs, keeping her little bitten hands for ever from picking and stealing. Putting her to sleep.

'I wished it. I wanted him to do it.'

He thought of Ghislaine asleep in her own bed, beached in the heaping sand-dunes of her yellow hair. Never again. Never. And Honey and Ghislaine twining together, twins for blondness and prettiness, with a wild innocence in their playing bred of sheer perversity. And Honey alone dancing before him in his song-and-dance hat. And the two golden beloved children destroying each other.

'Did she love him and he not want her?' asked Emily, who saw the world grandly and simply, as in a ballad.

('But I wanted it. I am to blame, too, I should have guessed, I should have protected him –')

'No. This is the way he was. He was a murderer.'

Morris suddenly realized: 'Then Emily is carrying a murderer's baby!'

They had fallen through a hole in time into a dimension of pure horror. Colour them gone, colour them all gone. For a moment, he felt as if he was being screwed intolerably on a huge frame and would go lucidly, rationally insane.

'We must go,' Emily said calmly. 'There is nothing we can do.'

'Honey –'

'Perhaps he isn't here.'

They shrank behind the open door on the landing at the sound of a footstep from above. The thin pencil line of the candle flame he carried came down the stairs before him. He held the candle high in his left hand. Cap and dark glasses were mislaid or lost. His hair trailed like mad Ophelia's and his eyes were too large for his head. The angles and planes of the skull were showing through the flesh. What was familiar about him seemed pared away, the daytime flesh carved off his bones so that he appeared to them, finally, naked and elementary and unknowable in the integrity of his own skeleton, in the night. Under his breath, he sang a song they could not hear.

He was cradling something in his right arm. As he drew nearer, Morris saw it was the plaster Christ. He did not see them, although he passed within a foot or two of them, but went into the room and pulled the door to behind him.

Consciousness ceased. Morris could not remember how they got out of the house. They moved in slow-motion, dreamy, tranced; when, in the open air, they stared at each other again, they were desperate and surprised, survivors from some shipwreck. Emily's skirt was torn and she had lost a shoe. He saw the moony glitter of the silver toenails on her left foot. There were cobwebs in her hair.

'The poor, poor girl,' she said. Then she doubled up and vomited again. Morris held her cold moist forehead until she finished and wiped her mouth.

'It is the baby, the baby,' she insisted, 'not that in there that makes me sick. I have been being sick a lot. It is the baby.' And then, in a joyful wail she could not control: 'Oh, I am so glad about my baby!'

But it is a murderer's baby! thought Morris. But she smiled, smiled her glorious smile and he realized that she was, indeed, glad that she was pregnant and that, in her mind, Honey by now had nothing to do with it. She was exultant. She smiled and smiled again. Helplessly, he blunted his mind against her opaque and impenetrable simplicity. She had decided to love her baby. That was all.

In the hardness of this simplicity, she said: 'There is a telephone box. I see it. We must call the police.'

'No,' he said. 'You can't do that. He's ill, he's defenceless.'

'They will look after him,' she said. 'We must get things straight. It is only right. For my baby's sake.'

She did not wait for him but set off on her own, unevenly, because one foot was bare. A single picture flashed again and again through Morris's mind – the Honey of the happy hat, dancing before him. And he remembered how they had embraced and he felt the wild beating of Honey's heart and then he had thrust him away. And was that why now the girl lay dead, the girl Morris had feared so much when she was alive, the girl he gave to Honey saying 'teach her a lesson'? Was she dead because he had rejected Honey? Did such things happen? Why was he bound to Honey – 'Am I my brother's keeper?' But Cain said that, treacherous Cain.

Emily entered the telephone box and lifted the receiver, to betray.

'No, Emily! No!'

He stumbled into a run to try and stop her but by the time he got to the telephone box she had already dialled the number and was speaking into the mouthpiece. He beat on the glass door with his fists in impotent fury. Nothing – could he do nothing at all? His fists unclenched and his teeth (oh why, why now?) screamed in a rising crescendo of pain in his head. There was nothing to be done, he realized in an aching tumult, except the one unimaginable thing.

'I must go back to him. But I can't, how can I . . .?'

He was sweating and shaking. He battled with his cowardice, trying to deny the choice which faced him. He could do the unimaginable thing; here was the single climactic thing, in all his life, when he need not be true to himself. He need not, at this moment, act like himself, but like a hero. Yet the old Morris died hard. The forces pulled him this way. Warring forces pulled him this way and that way.

To go back into the house, forsaking the clear light of the street lamps and the sweet clean breeze; to enter, Orpheus-like, the shadowed regions of death (Orpheus in the sepia engraving, straight nose, curls, harp, in the book in the auction room a million years ago) and, like Orpheus, to rescue or destroy a dear companion. Or to submit to his old self and stay outside and let the real world go storming in and stand there, weeping and shrugging, acknowledging its authority over him.

But where was the real world now? The image of it was the candle-lit room in the silent house and the girl under the tablecloth. And in this new dimension outside both time and space he, Morris, could truly be heroic.

'The world fell down around me when I was seven years old,' he thought. 'And now it has fallen down again and here I am, and am I brave enough to walk into the ruins?'

When the dust of the catastrophe cleared, he would be alone, alone as he had never been before, with only the new concept of himself as a hero to keep him company. And maybe that would be enough?

'And Honey is still Honey, somewhere, surely, though he is mad and can't be recognized. And I cannot betray him, even if Emily can. How can I betray him?'

So he made his choice and turned back. 'Good-bye,' he called over his shoulder to Emily, although she could not hear him, and then turned his face away from her. His feet fell slow and heavy. This morning, his feet had made sprightly, victory music, a quick march; but the morning had changed to night and the music to a slow march, the muffled single drumbeats of a cortège.

Emily came out of the telephone box and was taken at once with a new sickness. She knelt on the pavement, vomiting as if she would bring her heart up. She knelt in a pool of vomit.

Morris vanished into the shadows.

VIRAGO MODERN CLASSICS
&
CLASSIC NON-FICTION

The first Virago Modern Classic, *Frost in May* by Antonia White, was published in 1978. It launched a list dedicated to the celebration of women writers and to the rediscovery and reprinting of their works. Its aim was, and is, to demonstrate the existence of a female tradition in fiction, and to broaden the sometimes narrow definition of a 'classic' which has often led to the neglect of interesting novels and short stories. Published with new introductions by some of today's best writers, the books are chosen for many reasons: they may be great works of fiction; they may be wonderful period pieces; they may reveal particular aspects of women's lives; they may be classics of comedy or storytelling.

The companion series, Virago Classic Non-Fiction, includes diaries, letters, literary criticism, and biographies – often by and about authors published in the Virago Modern Classics.

'Good news for everyone writing and reading today' – *Hilary Mantel*

'A continuingly magnificent imprint' – *Joanna Trollope*

'The Virago Modern Classics have reshaped literary history and enriched the reading of us all. No library is complete without them' – *Margaret Drabble*

VIRAGO MODERN CLASSICS
&
CLASSIC NON-FICTION

Some of the authors included in these two series –

Elizabeth von Arnim, Dorothy Baker, Pat Barker, Nina Bawden,
Nicola Beauman, Sybille Bedford, Jane Bowles, Kay Boyle,
Vera Brittain, Leonora Carrington, Angela Carter, Willa Cather,
Colette, Ivy Compton-Burnett, E.M. Delafield, Maureen Duffy,
Elaine Dundy, Nell Dunn, Emily Eden, George Egerton,
George Eliot, Miles Franklin, Mrs Gaskell,
Charlotte Perkins Gilman, George Gissing,
Victoria Glendinning, Radclyffe Hall, Shirley Hazzard,
Dorothy Hewett, Mary Hocking, Alice Hoffman,
Winifred Holtby, Janette Turner Hospital, Zora Neale Hurston,
Elizabeth Jenkins, F. Tennyson Jesse, Molly Keane,
Margaret Laurence, Maura Laverty, Rosamond Lehmann,
Rose Macaulay, Shena Mackay, Olivia Manning, Paule Marshall,
F.M. Mayor, Anaïs Nin, Kate O'Brien, Olivia, Grace Paley,
Mollie Panter-Downes, Dawn Powell, Dorothy Richardson,
E. Arnot Robertson, Jacqueline Rose, Vita Sackville-West,
Elaine Showalter, May Sinclair, Agnes Smedley, Dodie Smith,
Stevie Smith, Nancy Spain, Christina Stead, Carolyn Steedman,
Gertrude Stein, Jan Struther, Han Suyin, Elizabeth Taylor,
Sylvia Townsend Warner, Mary Webb, Eudora Welty,
Mae West, Rebecca West, Edith Wharton, Antonia White,
Christa Wolf, Virginia Woolf, E.H. Young

THE PASSION OF NEW EVE

Angela Carter

'If you can imagine Baudelaire, Blake and Kafka getting together to describe America, you are well on the way to Carter's visionary and lurid world' – *The Times*

New York has become the City of Dreadful Night where dissolute Leilah performs a dance of chaos for Evelyn. But this young Englishman's fate lies in the arid desert where a many-breasted fertility goddess will wield her scalpel to transform him into the new Eve. This is the story of how Evelyn learns to be a woman – first in the brutal hands of Zero, the one-eyed, one-legged monomaniac poet; then through the gentle touch of the ancient Tristessa, the beautiful ghost of Hollywood past; and, finally, in a deserted Californian cave by the sea.

SEVERAL PERCEPTIONS

Angela Carter

Centre stage in Angela Carter's exuberant, unruly theatre of the imagination is the decadent Joseph, a twenty-two year old self-styled nihilist in search of life's meaning. He is watched over by his best friend Viv, the working-class dandy who loves good clothes and his mum; and Annie, his strangely enigmatic new neighbour who bears gifts of flowers and casseroles. The '60s are swinging and the beat of youth pulses with strange and strong passions. Joseph feels compelled to free a badger from the local zoo; sends a turd, airmail, to the President of America; and, accompanied by the strains of an old man's violin, celebrates New Year's Eve in a bewildering state of sexual discovery at an extraordinary revel – part Alice in Wonderland, part Dionysian.

Winner of the Somerset Maugham Award in 1968.

Now you can order superb titles directly from Virago

☐	Fireworks	Angela Carter	£6.99
☐	The Magic Toyshop	Angela Carter	£6.99
☐	Nothing Sacred	Angela Carter	£5.99
☐	The Passion of New Eve	Angela Carter	£6.99
☐	The Sadeian Woman: An Exercise in Cultural History	Angela Carter	£5.99
☐	Several Perceptions	Angela Carter	£6.99
☐	The Virago Book of Fairy Tales	Angela Carter	£7.99
☐	The Second Virago Book of Fairy Tales	Angela Carter	£7.99
☐	Wayward Girls and Wicked Women	Angela Carter	£6.99

Please allow for postage and packing: **Free UK delivery**.
Europe; add 25% of retail price; Rest of World; 45% of retail price.

To order any of the above or any other Virago titles, please call our
credit card orderline or fill in this coupon and send/fax it to:

Virago, 250 Western Avenue, London, W3 6XZ, UK.
Fax 0181 324 5678   Telephone 0181 3245516

☐ I enclose a UK bank cheque made payable to Virago for £ ....

☐ Please charge £ .... to my Access, Visa, Delta, Switch Card No.

☐☐☐☐☐☐☐☐☐☐☐☐☐☐☐☐☐☐☐

Expiry Date ☐☐☐☐   Switch Issue No. ☐☐

NAME (Block letters please) ....

ADDRESS ....

....

....

Postcode ....Telephone ....

Signature ....

Please allow 28 days for delivery within the UK. Offer subject to price and availability.

Please do not send any further mailings from companies carefully selected by Virago ☐